"If You Had Any Questions, You Could Have Asked Me.

"Instead of snooping behind my back."

"I thought you were hiding something to do with Alex," Sophie explained.

"You thought I was involved in Alex's disappearance? You slept with me, thinking I might be responsible? I thought we had something special, but you were just using me, weren't you?"

"Zach, I'm sorry," she said again.

"What were you planning to do? *Seduce* the information out of me?"

"You were so secretive. I just started to get suspicious. And while it started with wanting to seduce information out of you, it's not like that now. Please, Zach, please give me—us—another chance."

* * *

Something about the Boss... is part of the series Texas Cattleman's Club: The Missing Mogul— Love and scandal meet in Royal, Texas!

* * *

If you're on Twitter, tell us what you think of Harlequin Desire! #harlequindesire

Dear Reader,

When I was invited to participate in the Texas Cattleman's Club continuity, I was both deeply honoured and scared witless! :-) What do I, here in New Zealand, know about Texas? The best form of research, I've always found, is to read—and what better to read than previous Texas Cattleman's Club books to give me the texture and flavor of the people and the country that makes up this enduring continuity.

A continuity is, by its very nature, a group effort. From the concept and the development of the stories that comes directly from our editorial team, to the authors who bring the characters, setting and plotlines to life, we become a like-minded community that strives toward a joint goal—bringing you, our readers, the stories you love to read, again and again.

In *Something About the Boss...*, you will meet Sophie Beldon. Calm, capable, superefficient and totally unflappable...until, due to her boss's disappearance, she's forced to work with her biggest crush—her boss's work partner, dark, sexy and secretive Zach Lassiter. Their work-based relationship soon flares into something bigger than either of them can anticipate, with threads that can weave them together and have the equal potential to tear them apart, forever.

I hope you love reading this installment in the Texas Cattleman's Club: The Missing Mogul, and I wish you happy reading ahead through the rest of the continuity!

Best wishes, always,

Yvonne Lindsay

SOMETHING ABOUT THE BOSS...

—

YVONNE LINDSAY

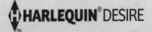
HARLEQUIN® DESIRE

Special thanks and acknowledgment to Yvonne Lindsay for her contribution to Texas Cattleman's Club: The Missing Mogul miniseries.

Recycling programs
for this product may
not exist in your area.

ISBN-13: 978-0-373-73265-4

SOMETHING ABOUT THE BOSS...

Printed in U.S.A.

YVONNE LINDSAY

New Zealand born, to Dutch immigrant parents, Yvonne Lindsay became an avid romance reader at the age of thirteen. Now, married to her "blind date" and with two fabulous children, she remains a firm believer in the power of romance. Yvonne feels privileged to be able to bring to her readers the stories of her heart. In her spare time, when not writing, she can be found with her nose firmly in a book, reliving the power of love in all walks of life. She can be contacted via her website, www.yvonnelindsay.com.

This one is for the amazing team at Harlequin who, I'm sure, often miss out on thanks for all you do in the foreground, the background and the playground. :-)

One

Sophie flew into the office five minutes later than usual. It drove her crazy to be late, for any reason. She'd woken way past her usual time and had had to forgo her morning coffee and bagel in an attempt to make up for it. With a vague wave at their receptionist and the skeleton staff already working at their stations in the open-plan office behind reception, Sophie went through to the executive office suite, smoothing her short blond bob with one hand.

She flung a glance at Zach's office door—it was open. Darn. He was already here. Despite her best efforts, Zach Lassiter had beaten her into the office, again. Not good. Not when she was doing her best to keep everything running on an even keel, and certainly not when she needed to do some snooping in his office. He was hiding something, she just knew it.

She dropped her shoulder bag on the corner of her

desk. The bag didn't quite make it, though, and it slid off the surface to fall silently onto the thick carpeting, its contents spilling at her feet.

"Damn!" The curse slipped from her lips and even now, though she hadn't lived under her mother's roof in more than four years, she felt the quiet reproof of her mother's gaze for dropping her standards so. They might have been poor, but her mother had always expected her to act like a lady.

She scrabbled to put everything back where it belonged—a place for everything and everything in its place; it had been her mantra for longer than she could remember. Her hand hovered over the photo she carried with her everywhere and she straightened with it still in her hand. They'd been so young, so innocent. Victims of circumstance.

Silently she renewed her vow to find her half-sister; Sophie owed it to them both. And she was getting closer. The latest report from the private investigator she'd hired to find her sister had listed a new possibility to explore. Thinking about it had kept her awake half the night, hence her sleeping past her alarm this morning.

A noise from behind her, from the kitchenette that she kept well stocked, sent a prickle of awareness tiptoeing between her shoulder blades.

"Cute kids."

Zach gave one of his lazy, killer smiles that always managed to send a bolt of longing straight to her gut, as he handed her a coffee. Sophie fought to quell the tremor that threatened to make her hand shake as she accepted the mug. She'd tried to shore up her defenses against her crazy attraction to him, but even after eighteen months she still failed miserably. Working in the same office space with him had been taxing enough, but now working directly for him—well, that was a whole new kettle of fish altogether.

"I'm supposed to be the one bringing you coffee," she said quietly. "Sorry I'm late."

"No problem. I was getting myself one. Is that you?" he asked gesturing to the photo in her hand.

It was the kind of snapshot that most kids had taken at some stage in their lives. Siblings, oldest behind, youngest in front. Gap-toothed smiles fixed on their freckled faces, hair pulled back into identical pigtails, bangs straight across their eyebrows. Oldest staring dead ahead, youngest—still baby-faced at age four—with eyes unfocused, distracted by whatever it was that day. Sophie certainly couldn't recall although she remembered well the sensation of her sister's bony shoulder beneath her hand, the steady warmth of Susannah's body standing close to hers, almost leaning into hers in that way she did when she wasn't entirely comfortable with a situation.

"Yes, me and my younger sister."

"Are you guys close?"

"Not anymore," she hedged.

Suzie's father, Sophie's much-adored stepdad, had died suddenly shortly after that photo had been taken. With their mother struggling to make ends meet, Suzie had gone to live with her father's sister. Financially independent and also recently widowed, Suzie's aunt had an open heart and open arms for her brother's only child. Contact between the two families had been severed almost immediately—deemed to be in the best interests of the girls at the time. It had been more than twenty years since they'd seen each other and Sophie still felt the emptiness inside, even though she'd long since learned how to mask it.

She thumbed the well-worn edge of the photo before tucking the picture back in her bag. She was doing what she could to reestablish contact with her sister. She had to be satisfied with that. She gave herself a mental shake and locked her handbag away in the bottom drawer of her desk. Even though this was downtown Royal, Texas, Sophie didn't take chances. It wasn't her way.

Clearly taking the hint that the subject of her sister was closed, Zach turned his attention to work.

"What's on your agenda today?"

Sophie briefly outlined what she had planned in her other boss's absence before asking, "Is there something else you need me to work on instead? None of this is urgent right now, especially with Alex still out of the office."

Out of the office. She gave an inward sigh. Some euphemism for missing. It had been over a month since her boss had simply disappeared off the face of the earth. Each morning she still hoped that she'd come in and find him in his office, his energetic personality filling the room, but each morning she was disappointed. The police were now involved in the hunt for Alex Santiago and his disappearance looked more sinister by the day.

"Any news from Sheriff Battle?" Zach asked.

She shook her head. Sophie had racked her brain trying to think of anything that could have been a clue to why Alex had gone, and where. But nothing had been out of the usual. The guy had disappeared the same way as he'd arrived in Royal, although with a great deal less fanfare. He was the kind of man who *made* things happen—things didn't happen *to* him. Which made his disappearance all the more puzzling. Surely someone had to know something. Someone, somewhere was keeping secrets, and Sophie had a worried feeling it might be Zach.

The muscles around his mouth tightened slightly, his only tell that something was bothering him. If anyone knew anything about Alex, it should have been Zach, as the two men had become firm friends in the time they'd worked together and shared office space. She watched him carefully. Zach Lassiter had a reputation for keeping his cards close to his chest and only letting you know what he thought you should know, when he thought you needed to know it.

The man was locked tighter than the vault at Fort Knox. Goodness only knew he'd remained impervious to the subtle and not-so-subtle questioning from local men and women alike. All anyone knew about him was that just under two years ago he'd arrived here in Royal with his own investment company and a knack for turning high-risk investment opportunities into sure fortunes. When Alex Santiago had arrived a couple of months later and set up his venture capital business, they'd created the perfect successful partnership.

It hadn't taken a whole lot of research to find out that Zach Lassiter had been married, not when his ex still called him almost every day, although Sophie had been unable to find any photos online that included Anna Lassiter. It also hadn't taken a lot of poking to discover that Zach's knack for turning high-risk investment opportunities into gold had started several years ago with an investment firm in Midland.

But the man himself? What made him tick, what drove him? There was nothing. Dark good looks and urbane charm aside, he could be hiding anything beneath that smooth, sophisticated exterior. It was whether that "anything" involved Alex's disappearance that Sophie wanted to find out.

"What? Have I got something on my face?" Zach asked, reminding Sophie she was staring.

Color flooded her cheeks and she ducked her head. "No, sorry, I was just distracted for a minute."

The phone on Sophie's desk chimed discreetly. Zach's line. He usually took his own calls, but since he was here with her, Sophie reached for the handset.

"Zach Lassiter's office, this is Sophie speaking."

"I can't reach Zach on his phone. Is he there? Put me through to him," the woman's querulous voice demanded, belatedly adding, "Please."

"One moment please, I'll see if he's free to take your call." Recognizing the voice, and putting the woman on hold, Sophie said, "It's your ex-wife. You're not answering your cell phone. Do you want to take it?"

"Of course." He patted the breast pocket of his jacket. "I must have left my cell in the car again." He fished his keys out of his pocket and handed them to Sophie. "When you have a free moment, could you get it for me?"

"Sure," she said, taking the keys and trying desperately to ignore the buzz of attraction that warmed her skin as his fingertips brushed her palm.

She watched as he walked back to his office and heard the deep murmur of his voice through his closed door as he picked up the call. Not for the first time she wondered about the relationship Zach had with Anna Lassiter. She could count on one finger the number of people she knew who were still on speaking terms with their exes, let alone *daily* speaking terms. As far as she could ascertain, he and Anna had been divorced for nearly two years. She shook her head. He had to still be in love with the woman. Why else would he devote so much time to her?

Sophie fought to quell the pang of envy that struck deep in her chest. What would it be like to be the object of Zach's devotion? His closed demeanor aside, the man was sex on legs. Or maybe it was that very aloofness that made him so appealing to her. She took a sip of her rapidly cooling coffee. No, it was more visceral than that. To use a more colloquial expression, the man was prime beef. It was no hardship to imagine the lean, hard-muscled lines of his body beneath the tailored suits he wore.

A tiny thrill coursed down the length of her spine, setting a tingle up in her lower back. Lord, she had it bad. Just thinking about him was enough to send her pulse up a few notches and a flush of awareness to heat all those secret parts of her body that were hidden by her office clothes.

Combine a killer physique with a handsomely chiseled face, expensively cropped jet-black hair, green eyes that looked straight through you and a mind as sharp as a tack, and he became a very appealing package. From the first day he'd walked through the front door of the professional suite and taken up the spare office next to Alex's, Sophie had been mesmerized by him. He carried himself with an air of confidence that made it clear that he was there to succeed at whatever he turned his hand to. And succeed he did. His investment advice had made his client list an exceptionally large and equally wealthy one. Some even said he had a Midas touch and, if his address on the outskirts of town was any indicator, he certainly knew how to put his money to good use.

She also knew that you didn't get anywhere without hard work and dedication and if she didn't apply some

of that to the list of things she had to do today, she'd
have to answer to Alex when he came back. If he came
back, whispered a small voice in the back of her head.

Zach hung up from the call and just for a moment
allowed himself the indulgence of resting his head in
his hands. He was worried about Anna. She'd always
been high-strung, but right now she was acting as if
she was stretched to the breaking point. He had to do
something, and do it soon. Her parents still insisted
there was nothing wrong with her, keeping their heads
in the sand regarding any potential mental imbalance.

Their refusal to admit to her instability wasn't doing
her any favors. She needed help—professional help—
and it was up to him to find it for her. Drawing in a
deep breath, Zach straightened and booted up his laptop, opening a search window. Before long he had a
list of people and places to contact. He'd do more research tonight.

Zach pressed his fingertips against his closed eyelids.
He felt so damned responsible. He should never have
married Anna, never bowed down to her father's—his
boss's—unstintingly direct pressure to court his only
child.

Sure, Zach had been attracted to her. She was blonde
and beautiful and had an air of delicacy about her that
had appealed to the caveman inside him in a way he'd
never experienced before. But he'd been all wrong for
her. She'd needed someone less driven, more devoted.
Certainly someone less earthy. It hadn't taken long for
the fragility to wear thin, for him to feel trapped. Then,
just when they'd begun separation proceedings, she'd
discovered she was pregnant and it had become far too
late to walk away. He'd tried to do his best by her—

after all, he'd vowed to her before man and God that he'd stand by her through all that life could throw at them.

But life had thrown them a complete curveball with the death of their baby son. And while Zach had learned to hide his pain beneath a shell of self-preservation, Anna's guilt over the car wreck that had taken ten-month-old Blake's life had seen her spiral deeper and deeper into depression.

"Zach? Is everything all right?"

He hadn't even heard Sophie come into his office. He snapped to attention. "Sure, everything's fine. Just a bit tired is all."

"I found your phone. You'd left it connected to your hands-free kit."

She slid it across the desk toward him, the screen letting him know exactly how many calls he'd missed from Anna. He sighed. Tonight he would definitely make some decisions. It was past time.

"Thanks, I appreciate it."

He lifted his gaze and met Sophie's. She was a sight for sore eyes, with her cute blond bob and those warm, whiskey-brown eyes of hers. Today had been the first time he'd seen her approach anything outside of her usual unflappable mien, when she'd arrived a few minutes late. He kind of liked seeing her a little off-kilter. It made her seem more human, more approachable.

She always looked immaculate—her clothes well cut but not flashy—and he'd long envied Alex her calm, capable efficiency. As Alex's executive assistant, she kept the place running like clockwork, keeping an overview of not only all the pies Alex had his thumb in but every aspect of every pie. You had to admire a mind that could compartmentalize and draw information out on command the way hers did. In Alex's absence, the cracks would surely have started to show by now without her talents.

Zach hadn't wasted a second on availing himself of her skills over the past month, when it had become clear that Alex's disappearance was more than the temporary foray they'd all thought he might have indulged in. With the police now handling the disappearance of his good friend, Zach had doubled his workload, juggling both his own clients' portfolios and Alex's venture capital concerns. Without Sophie he'd have dropped the ball by now.

He really ought to show her some appreciation. He spoke out loud before thinking on the subject long enough to talk himself out of it.

"Sophie, you've been a godsend these past weeks. I couldn't have managed it all without your help. I know you've been putting in some long hours and I'd like to make it up to you. How about dinner at Claire's at the end of the week? Sound good?"

"You don't need to do that, Zach. I'm only doing my job—one I'm very well compensated for."

"I know, but I am grateful and I'd like to show it. I'll make the reservation today, and Sophie? I won't take no for an answer."

She gave a little laugh, the sound a gurgle of amusement that removed the last of the dark cloud in the back of his mind and pulled an answering smile across his lips.

"Well, when you put it like that, what can I say? Thank you, I'll look forward to it."

He watched her turn and leave his office, noted the way the fabric of her straight skirt skimmed her hips and pulled across her buttocks with each no-nonsense step. An unwanted pull of desire tugged deep inside him and he forced himself to avert his gaze. Acknowledging that Sophie Beldon was an attractive woman was one thing, but actually doing something about it was off-limits. They worked together, and he didn't want to jeopardize that. Too much hinged on them continuing to work in synchronicity until Alex's return. Besides, look at the disaster of his last work-related relationship. It wasn't something he was in a hurry to repeat.

He'd asked her out to dinner to express his gratitude, that was all. There couldn't be any more to it than that—no matter what his clamoring libido insisted to the contrary.

Two

"Thank you, I shall look forward to it?" What on earth had she been thinking? The words played over and over in her head, so stilted, so... Argh! Why couldn't she have come back with something witty or sophisticated? Something that might have attracted his interest just that little bit more.

This was further proof that a man like Zach Lassiter was out of her league, Sophie castigated herself as she settled at her desk and tried to force her mind back to analyzing the projection figures that had come in on Alex's latest venture. They made for interesting reading and her fingers itched to compile her report. But even as she started entering the data into her computer, her mind kept flicking back to Zach's dinner invitation.

Her pulse skipped an excited beat. Claire's was not your run-of-the-mill restaurant and the prices there reflected that. She'd only ever made reservations there for Alex and his various business contacts—she'd never had the good fortune to dine there herself. Sophie quelled an inner squeal of delight and reminded herself she was a sage twenty-eight years old, not a giddy teenager. Besides, this wasn't anything like a date. It was a work-related bonus, that's all. And the sooner she started believing it, the better.

When her phone rang, she was glad for the interruption to her thoughts, even more so when she heard who was on the end of the line.

"Lila," she greeted one of her dearest friends, "how are you?"

Lila Hacket had been making a strong name for herself in set production design in Los Angeles. Sophie was so very proud of her for carving out such success in that competitive world. A world as far from hers as it was probably possible to get, when you thought about it. When Lila had been in Royal to work on a movie being filmed there, the two women had had scant opportunity to catch up beyond the barbecue Lila's father had hosted last month. Even then it had been so packed they'd had little chance to really talk. Except about Zach Lassiter, that was. Strange how he kept coming up in her thoughts and conversations, Sophie mused before pushing him to the back of her mind.

"I'm feeling just fine, thank you," Lila said. "Under the circumstances."

Sophie could hear the grin that was undoubtedly painted on her friend's face. She could always tell when Lila had news she was itching to share.

"Circumstances? C'mon, spill," she demanded. "I know you too well for you to keep a secret from me for long."

"I have news." Lila chuckled.

Sophie's lips twitched into a broad smile. "You and Sam? I knew it! There always were too many sparks between the two of you."

"More than sparks, we're getting married."

Sophie let go a shriek of delight, then, remembering where she was, rapidly tried to calm herself. "Congratulations! When?"

"Last Saturday of the month. We're having it on the Double H. We just want to keep it simple and low-key."

"And your father agreed to that? Low-key really isn't his style, is it?"

Lila laughed. "No, you're right, but I'm standing firm on this. Close friends and family only. Besides, any more than that will probably wear me out, seeing as how I'm pregnant and all."

Sophie's breath caught in her throat as the news sank in. Excitement and sheer joy swelled up within her.

"Pregnant? Oh my, that was quick. Congratulations again, that's wonderful news."

"Not so quick, actually, I'm just over four months along."

"You've been holding out on me," Sophie accused her in a teasing tone. "We'll need to talk this out face-to-face, I think."

"Definitely. Oh—" Lila hesitated for a moment and Sophie heard her draw in a deep breath "—and it's twins."

"Twins! How long have you known?"

"About the twins? Not all that long, although I have known for a while about being pregnant. I just needed some time to come to terms with it. To sort out in my own mind what I was doing next. It's part of why I came home last month."

Sophie could easily imagine what it was like to face

raising a child on her own. Although Lila's position, both financial and social, was vastly different from what Sophie's mother's had been. Lila would never have been short of support, emotional or monetary, which was a luxury Sophie's mom had never had. She pushed those sad thoughts aside, wanting instead to give her full focus to her friend's exciting announcement.

"I'm so very happy for you, Lila. A wedding and twin babies to look forward to? It's wonderful, *wonderful* news. You have to let me host your baby shower, please! My mind is already brimming with ideas."

"Are you sure it won't be too much work for you? You've got so much on your plate already, especially with your boss still gone."

Sophie made a shushing sound to her friend. "Don't be ridiculous. It would be an honor to host your shower. You just leave it all to me."

"Thank you, Sophie."

"You're very welcome. It's the least I can do for you. So does this mean you'll be staying in Royal?"

"Sam's offered to relocate to L.A. with me, to set up a branch of Gordon Construction there, but we're holding off making a decision until after the babies are born." She gave another breathy laugh. "I still can't believe it. Babies!"

"It's going to be amazing," Sophie reassured her. "But are you sure we're talking about the same Sam Gordon?"

Sam had vocalized his thoughts about a woman's place being in the home on more than one occasion. In fact he'd been one of the most vociferous in opposition to the new child-care center at the Texas Cattleman's Club when it was initially proposed.

"Just goes to show even a leopard can change his

spots with the right motivation," Lila answered, and Sophie could hear the happiness ringing through her voice. "So, tell me. You haven't done anything silly about what we talked about last month, have you? I'm worried about you."

Sophie huffed out a small breath and lowered her voice. "To even have an opportunity would be a fine thing. No, don't worry, I still haven't been able to do any snooping around Zach Lassiter. I'm quite safe."

Their conversation turned to more general matters and after Sophie replaced her handset on the cradle, she took a moment to hug Lila's exciting news to herself. Her friend had been fiercely independent for so long, had carved a strong career for herself against some pretty tough odds, and now here she was—on the precipice of a whole new adventure in her life. Marriage to a man she clearly loved with all her generous heart, and expecting his babies.

Truth be told, Sophie felt a little envious of Lila. What would it be like, she wondered, to carry the baby of the man you loved? Without realizing it her eyes strayed to Zach's closed office door. She shook her head. She wasn't in love with Zach Lassiter. Of course she wasn't.

Sure, she was attracted to him. Majorly attracted to him, even though she had some niggling suspicions that he knew more about Alex's disappearance than he was letting on. But she didn't know him. Not really. Certainly not enough to begin contemplating what it would be like to have his child, and certainly not enough to fully trust him. Even so, she couldn't help wondering what it would be like to be the sole focus of his attention. To feel not only his gaze upon her, but his lips, his hands, his body, as well. Zach stood a good six inches

taller than her own five and a half feet and he had a
strong build. How he found the time to stay in shape
with the hours he spent in the office or out on business
calls she didn't know, but it was easy to see in the way
he walked and in the fit of his clothing that he took
care of himself.

She could only begin to imagine what it would be
like to trace the outlines of his muscles from shoulder
to chest…and lower. Tendrils of heat spread from the
pit of her belly and made her insides clench on a surge
of need so intense it almost made her gasp out loud.

Sophie pushed away from her desk and went through
to the kitchenette to grab a glass of water. She took a
long drink of the chilled liquid, but it did little to quell
the turmoil in her body. She was being ridiculous. A
woman like her was not Zach Lassiter's type. She lacked
the refinement he'd surely expect in his women. Not that
anyone ever saw him out with a woman on his arm. He
was as closed and careful about his relationships, if he
had them, as he was about everything else in his life.

It made her wonder again just how much he knew
about Alex Santiago's disappearance. Unlike everyone
else, he hadn't openly speculated on where Alex could
be. Did that mean that he knew something and was
keeping it secret, even from the police? Sophie shook
her head slightly. She didn't want to contemplate it.
Surely Zach wouldn't withhold vital information from
what was now a police investigation.

Zach appeared in the doorway, a sheaf of papers in
his hand and a worried frown on his forehead.

"Did you w-want me for something?" she asked, her
voice a little wobbly.

An inner groan tore through her. Want her? Like she
wanted him? She'd have to work harder to guard her

tongue. She turned away to reach for a mug from the cupboard so he wouldn't see the twin spots of color she just knew would be glowing in her cheeks the way they always did when she was uncomfortable.

"Yeah, can you come into my office when you're finished in here? I've been going over the pitch we're sending out for potential investors in the Manson project. I need you to help me fine-tune some things."

"Sure, I'll be there right away. Coffee?"

"Thanks," he replied, already walking away.

Sophie quelled the sigh that built in her chest. Yes, he wanted her all right. For work, not for play.

Her nerves were stretched raw by the end of the week. She and Zach had worked late most nights, he even later than she, and he'd beaten her into the office each morning, as well. Even getting half the chance to check around his office was impossible. Lila certainly would have no worries on that score.

Sophie knew it was important that they get their pitch perfect for the Manson project. It was something that Alex had started before he had disappeared. It had become a matter of pride for both her and Zach to deliver no less than Alex would have when it came to sourcing investors for Ally Manson's start-up. The seventeen-year-old prodigy was an IT genius and Alex had been hugely excited by the opportunity to launch her idea of a nationwide computer-assisted home disability network. Astute investors at the outset would be integral to her success and, by association, theirs, as well.

For all the hard work and long hours they'd been putting in, Sophie was still surprised that Zach was spending so much extra time at the office, and most of it with his door closed. A couple of times she'd entered his office, only to hear him abruptly put his caller on hold or close his laptop so she wouldn't see what was on his screen. There was something going on that wasn't quite right, but she couldn't put her finger on it.

But it wasn't his hours that had unsettled her the most this week. It was just him. For some stupid reason, Lila's news had triggered something in her that had begun to blow out of proportion. She'd been able to control her attraction to him without any issues over the past eighteen months, even though they'd started working together more closely since Alex had disappeared. Now, though, the proximity was driving her crazy and affecting her concentration when it was more important than ever that she be on the ball.

It was as if her hormones had gone into overdrive, as if her friend's pregnancy had triggered a persistent reminder that Sophie was twenty-eight, painfully single and childless—and that time wouldn't forever be on her side. Her body remained in a heightened state of awareness even when she wasn't around Zach—but when she was, it was a hundred times worse.

He only had to brush past her for every cell in her body to spring to aching, and embarrassingly eager, attention. And her dreams…she didn't even want to think about them, or about waking—hot, sweaty and wanting in the worst way.

Several times this week she'd battled with canceling tonight's dinner but some masochistic inner demon stopped her whenever she found the words to tell him their date was off. But it wasn't a date, was it? It was a reward, a bonus. He'd made it clear in his invitation he wanted to say thank-you for her work. Technically, she'd earned it. Still, the prospect of an evening in his company was winding her as tight as a spring and her constant battle with herself had worn her defenses ragged.

Sophie shut down her computer at five-thirty and slid her backup drive into the side pocket of her bag. She planned to have a long, hot, invigorating shower and take her time over getting ready for this evening. She was going to enjoy herself, dammit. He was an attractive, well-educated and erudite male. Tonight was a reward for her hard work. She had earned every second of it and would savor every bite of what would no doubt be a delicious meal.

"Everything still okay for this evening? I thought I'd pick you up at your place around seven-thirty."

Zach's voice cut through her resolve like a hot knife through butter. She couldn't do it. She couldn't sit opposite him over an intimate meal and not be driven totally crazy with wanting him. She'd be hopelessly uncomfortable and make some stupid mistake, like letting him know how she felt, and no doubt he'd end up embarrassed for her. It would be a kindness to both of them to avoid being in that situation altogether.

"About tonight," she started.

"I've made our reservation for eight," he continued before stopping to give her a sharp, assessing look. "You're not pulling out on me, are you? Thinking about dinner at Claire's tonight has been the only thing that's kept me going through the TV dinners and takeout all week."

"Yes, I... Oh, um, no," she vacillated. "There's no need to pick me up. I can meet you there."

"What kind of a gentleman would I be if I didn't collect you? My mama would be ashamed." He gave her a cheeky smile, then rattled off her address. "That's right, isn't it?"

She gave a brief nod.

"Good, I'll see you at seven-thirty."

He was gone and out the door before she could say another word. The faint chime of the elevator in the outer reception area galvanized her into action. If she didn't hurry, she wouldn't have time to gather her wits together for tonight, let alone present herself respectably.

Forty-five minutes later, she surveyed the underwear she'd chosen to wear for tonight. *Respectable* was the last word on her mind. She'd bought the tiny scraps of fabric during a girls' day out with her friend Mia Hughes, who worked as Alex's housekeeper. The pale-green silk had looked stunning against her ivory skin and the texture had felt deliciously sinful. The half-cup bra made it the perfect piece to wear beneath the deep-V-necked teal dress she'd bought for a "sometime" special occasion but hadn't yet had the opportunity to wear. Like the underwear, she'd bought it on impulse—something she rarely did after a childhood of poverty—and tonight seemed perfect to wear it for the first time. Armored with the expensive threads, she would feel like a million dollars—and right now she needed all the strength she could get.

Sophie luxuriated as long as she could under the stinging-hot spray of her shower, lathering her body twice with the expensive scented shower gel Lila had sent to her on her last birthday and which she saved only for special occasions. As she dragged her washcloth over her breasts, she felt her nipples pebble in anticipation of the evening ahead.

As conflicted as she felt about tonight's dinner, she knew one thing very clearly in her mind. She wanted Zach Lassiter with an ache that went straight to her core, and if all she could have of him was this meal together, then she was going to make the most of it.

By the time she'd toweled off, styled her hair and applied her makeup, she felt almost bulletproof. It felt decadently wicked sliding into the tiny panties and hooking the bra before stepping into her dress and shimmying it up her body. She cast an eye at the clock beside her bed. Darn, she was cutting it close. Sophie reached for the zipper and started to tug it upward while slipping her feet into the killer heels she'd bought with her dress, but the zipper halted in its tracks.

She squirmed, trying alternately to tug it down or ease it up. Blasted thing was stuck fast and no matter how much she wriggled, it just wouldn't budge. She tried to ease the gown off her shoulders but quickly gave that up as a bad idea. The dress was designed to be a skintight fit. There was no way she was going to get out of this one easily. What to do, what to do? She gave the tab on the zipper another jiggle, but still no luck.

This kind of thing did not happen to her. She was the consummate swan, gliding effortlessly across the lake of her life—outwardly, anyway. Control was the foundation of her life. Being at the mercy of something as inane as a stuck zipper was not something she was used to, not from this end, anyway.

But then again, the past week had been an exercise in levels of frustration she'd never experienced before. She huffed a sigh of exasperation. Zach would be here any minute now and, of course, right on cue, the doorbell rang.

Three

Zach pressed the doorbell again. He had said seven-thirty, hadn't he? He checked the TAG Heuer on his wrist. Yep, he was on time. He stepped back from the door and checked the side window. Lights were on inside and, yes, right there he saw a flash of movement through the crack in the drapes.

The door slowly opened.

"I'm sorry to keep you waiting," Sophie said, her light-brown eyes looking bigger and sexier than ever with the smoky makeup she wore.

"No problem, we have half an hour until our reservation." He hesitated, waiting a second for her to invite him in, but when no invitation was forthcoming he continued, "So, shall we head out?"

She gave him an awkward smile. "Yes, well, maybe in a minute or two. I've got a bit of a problem with my dress."

"Anything I can help with?"

Her dress? Maybe that explained why she wasn't opening the door fully and was talking to him with just her head popped around its edge.

Sophie sighed. "I think you might have to."

Huh. Well, there was no need for her to sound so eager, he thought. He waited again for her to open the door wider and to invite him inside. Still, she didn't move.

"Is this something we can fix here on the doorstep?" he inquired.

"Oh, no. No, of course not. You'd better come in."

She looked flustered, something he wasn't used to seeing in her. He raised his eyebrows slightly and, taking the hint, she finally eased the door wide enough for him to pass through. She closed it behind her, keeping her back to the door.

She was as skittish as a newborn colt. He wondered what had gotten her so riled up.

"It's my dress," she started, then stopped just as suddenly and worried her lower lip with her teeth.

His eyes were caught and mesmerized by the action. Sophie's lips were slick with gloss, several shades richer than what she normally wore to the office, he noted, and the color made him think of candy apples and all their sugary sweetness. Would she taste like that, too, if he nibbled on her lip the way she was doing right now?

Zach dragged his gaze from her mouth and from the forbidden thoughts she incited in him. She was strictly off-limits. What had she been talking about again? Yeah, that was right. Her dress.

"What's wrong with it? You look great to me," he said, letting his eyes skim over her.

Oh, yeah, she was the full package tonight. Her hair sat smooth and sleek in its unassuming bob. Fine, pale-blond hair that made his hand itch to reach out and feel if it was as silky soft as it looked. Desire hit hard and hot, driving a surge of lust straight to his groin. He fought to control it. This wasn't what tonight was supposed to be about. He firmed his jaw and wrestled his libido back under control, right up until she turned around, exposing the long ivory column of her back.

"My zipper. It's stuck. I think I've caught it on the lining. Do you think you can work it loose for me?"

Think? The woman expected him to think? Without realizing it, his hands moved to her back. One knuckle grazed against her warm skin. He felt her flinch beneath his touch.

"Sorry," he muttered and forced himself to concentrate on closing his fingers on the delicate tab of the zipper.

"Do you think you'll be able to work it loose?" she asked over her shoulder. "I'd hate to have to rip the dress."

He quelled a groan at the image of doing just that. Of ripping the dress from her slender form and exposing more than the hint of sheer green confection that was masquerading as underwear beneath her gown. If that was the back of her bra, he could only begin to imagine how alluring the front would be. On second thought, better not to imagine it, or his current discomfort would be nothing compared to what his body would do next.

"Sure," he ground out through gritted teeth. "Just give me a minute."

His knuckle brushed against her skin again. This time she didn't flinch, but he could see the reaction to his touch as tiny goose bumps rose in a scatter across her skin.

"I'm going to have to pull your dress down a bit,"

he said, warning her of his intention to hold the fabric firmly against her as he pulled the tab gently up.

There, he could feel the teeth letting go their grip on the smooth silk lining of the dress. He was almost sorry when the tab pulled free and he slid it up, closing that enticing view of her back and the band of her sheer bra.

"You're all set," he said, dropping his hands to his sides and stepping back from her. "And you look amazing."

"Oh, thank you," Sophie said, turning around to face him.

"Shall we go?" he suggested, eager now to put them in a position where they were surrounded by other people and where he wouldn't have to continually fight this urge to reach out to pull her to him and find out just how good those candy-apple lips tasted after all.

"Let me get my bag."

He looked around the apartment as she went into what he assumed was her bedroom. He liked what she'd created here. Despite its compact size the apartment had a light, airy feel to it—the furnishings combining a few good pieces with what were obviously refurbished yard-sale finds. It felt like a home. More so than his expertly furnished mansion on the outskirts of town. He loved living there, but it lacked the small touches that made a place more than just somewhere to eat and sleep. Mind you, for the amount of time he'd spent there lately, what did it matter? Besides, it was a prime investment. One he wouldn't hesitate to flick off when he was ready to move on or when the market was right. He didn't like to attach sentiment to assets the way his parents did. You never got ahead that way.

"I'm ready. Sorry for the delay, Zach."

She'd replenished her lip gloss while she'd been in

her room and looked so incredibly perfect from head to toe it was difficult to equate the woman in front of him with the slightly nervy creature who'd greeted him when he'd arrived. Women. He'd never understand them fully, nor did he really want to. Who had the time? But he certainly was in the right frame of mind to appreciate this one.

He guided her outside and waited on the path while she locked the front door, then escorted her to his gleaming black Cadillac CTS-V Coupe.

"New car?" Sophie inquired as he held open the passenger door for her.

"Not so new, but it's my fun car. For weekends and special occasions only," he said before closing the door on the inviting view of her slender legs.

He settled himself in the driver's seat and started up the engine, allowing the growl of the 6.2-liter V8 engine to course through him for just a moment.

"You like it?" he said with boyish enthusiasm.

"It certainly looks and sounds sleek and fast, but somehow I would never have pictured you driving something like this," she commented as she fastened her seat belt.

"No, why so?"

"With your reputation, I'd have picked you for European flash."

"My reputation?" He raised an eyebrow.

"For being a risk taker. I would have thought your idea of a fun car would be some imported speed machine."

He smiled. "No, proudly American all the way, that's me."

She was easy company on the drive to Claire's, not being one of those women who felt the need to fill empty space with constant idle chatter. By the time they entered the restaurant, he felt it safe enough to lay his hand at the small of her back without worrying that it would trigger a wave of heat and desire. He couldn't have been more wrong.

The instant his hand rested against the fabric of her dress, he could sense the warmth of her skin through its fine weave. The effect was more of a tsunami, threatening to swamp him. This was ridiculous, he thought as they were promptly shown to their table. He worked with Sophie every day. She was attractive, he'd always found her so, but he'd never had this kind of trouble keeping his attraction under control before.

He'd also never been quite this close to her before, never touched her, never smelled the light fragrance that trailed her now—a scent that reminded him of summer and roses and long hot aching nights. Maybe this was the real reason he'd envied his friend his capable assistant. Maybe it had nothing to do with her efficiency and all too much to do with the fact he hadn't been laid in far, far too long. He'd have to remedy that. For now, though, he had to exert his self-control—and remind himself that Sophie was off-limits.

They sat at the table, Sophie refusing an aperitif when the waiter offered.

"Did you want to have a glass of wine with dinner?" Zach asked as he perused the menu once the waiter had left.

"Sure, just one."

"Not much of a drinker, then?"

"No, I don't like losing control."

For a second there she looked surprised that she'd admitted as much. Zach gave her a nod.

"I know what you mean. It can bring out the best and the worst in people."

She smiled back at him, relief evident in her eyes.

"I'm glad you understand. Most people just think I'm some kind of control freak."

"I've seen you at work. I *know* you're a control freak," he teased gently.

A light flush colored her cheeks and she ducked her head, her short blond hair swinging forward to obstruct his view of her face as she put her attention to studying her menu.

"Anything in particular take your fancy?" he asked. "I know the steak is always good here."

"I've never been here before, but it all looks good to me."

"Did you want an appetizer?"

"No, I'll save myself for dessert."

"Ah," he said, "a sweet tooth, huh? I didn't know that about you."

"I would think there's a lot you don't know about me."

Her tone was slightly quelling, but Zach was nothing if not challenged by her statement. He noticed the exact second she realized the light of that challenge had reflected in his eyes.

"Not that I expect you to know anything about me, that is," she said, her voice flustered.

"I'd like to know more about you," he answered, closing his menu and laying it on the crisp white linen of the tablecloth. "We work together. There's no reason why we can't be friends also."

Sophie swallowed. There was a determined set to his jaw that she knew from watching him at work meant he wasn't going to let this go. Why, oh why had she been so careless with her tongue? From the second she'd agreed to this dinner she'd been off balance. Could she be friends with someone like Zach? She very much doubted it; especially considering how *unfriendlike* she'd felt when he'd ever so slightly touched her while rescuing her dress from the voracious teeth of the zipper.

She'd all but melted at the unintentional caress, and had had to draw on every last ounce of self-control to stifle the gasp that had threatened to expose her reaction to his touch. No, *friendly* was the last word she'd ever employ to describe how he made her feel.

Could she be friends with him, though? Honestly?

It would be tantamount to torture. But worse, how on earth could she explain *that* to him? She took a deep breath and let it go slowly before speaking. "I'm pretty boring, really."

"You think so?" he answered, cocking his head and locking those startlingly green eyes of his onto her like twin lasers.

She squirmed a little in her seat, and immediately regretted the action as she became even more aware of the silky softness of her underthings against her skin and of the way the silk lining of her dress whispered against her body.

"Well, by comparison to you, for example," she deflected, quite neatly she thought, right up until he let loose with a rich belt of laughter.

"Oh, Sophie, you couldn't be more wrong. I've been told I live to work. There's not much more boring than that."

Even though he joked at his own expense, she could see the light of an old hurt lingering in the back of his gaze. Compassion flooded her. A man in his early thirties, in his prime both mentally and physically, living to work? It was sad. Something must have shown on her face, because he sobered and reached across the table to grasp her hand.

"Don't worry about me," he said, his voice dropping intimately.

Oh, she wasn't worried about him, not exactly. Of more immediate concern was the crazy flip-flop her stomach did as his thumb lightly stroked the inside of her palm. She gently pulled her hand away from his, relief and regret fighting for supremacy as he made no move to stop her.

"What makes you think I'm worried?" she asked, a note of defense in her voice.

"You have the most expressive face," he answered, his eyes not shifting an inch. "It's easy to see when something's troubling you."

As long as that was all he could see, she thought worriedly. What if he could see the longing she felt every time she looked at him? A man like Zach Lassiter was so far out of her league it wasn't even funny. But a girl could dream, couldn't she?

"There's not much that troubles me," Sophie said, closing her menu and placing it in front of her. She could barely concentrate on the culinary delights the pages offered. It wouldn't matter what she ordered, it was bound to be delicious.

"But you're worried about Alex, aren't you? I can see it on your face every morning when you arrive in the office and he's not there."

"Aren't you?" she countered. "He's your friend as well as your colleague. Aren't you worried about where he is, what might have happened to him?"

"Sure I am," Zach replied. "I feel frustrated I can't do more. The only thing I know I *can* do is keep all those plates he had spinning from falling down so that when he comes back everything will still be as it should."

"Is that why you're in the office so early each morning and don't leave until after I do?" Sophie asked without thinking.

He looked startled at her question and his eyes became slightly shuttered before he replied. "Yeah, there's a lot going on right now."

"Can I take more of your load off you?" she offered.

"No, of course not. You already are the glue that holds the office together. No one could expect more of you than you already give. In fact, let's make that the end of the subject of work. We're here tonight because I wanted to thank you for everything you've done, not discuss how you can do more."

He smiled at that last sentence but Sophie could tell it was a deflection. She'd been wondering what it was that was keeping him in the office for such long hours. He was right, she did keep the office running, and she knew exactly what stage each of Alex's projects had been at before he'd disappeared. Unless Zach had suddenly become wildly incompetent, he should have been able to handle everything—his own portfolios included— within normal business hours, which made her wonder: What was he really up to?

Four

She reached for her water glass and took a tiny sip, letting the cool water slide down her throat while her mind worked overtime. The mere fact that he hadn't sent more work her way for all the extra hours he was putting in was a glaring red flag to her. Why hadn't she seen that earlier?

Her work had always increased incrementally depending on Alex's output. Zach was doing something he didn't want her to know about, he had to be. She was almost certain of it. But it was anyone's guess what, exactly, that was. Could he somehow be involved in Alex's disappearance? Was he actively hiding his tracks? The questions were never far from the back of her mind, even though she didn't want to believe Zach was entangled in whatever had led to Alex virtually vanishing off the face of the earth.

There had to be some way she could find out.

"I do appreciate your hard work, Sophie," he said,

dragging her attention back. "And I know you put in some very long hours. Doesn't your boyfriend object?"

"I don't have a boyfriend," she answered, feeling warm color flood her cheeks again.

Silently she cursed her fair complexion. There was only one man she was interested in and he was sitting right opposite her. What would he say, she wondered, if she told him exactly that? She fought back a smile. He'd probably make some excuse to draw the evening to a close early.

"I'm surprised. You're a very attractive woman," Zach said seriously, ensnaring her in his gaze like a predatory cat with its prey.

"Thank you," she said, dipping her head.

"So, no boyfriend, huh? What do you like to do in your spare time if you don't have a significant other filling it with you?"

"I read a lot, romances mostly and the occasional crime thriller." She shrugged. "And I keep house, see friends. The usual things."

"Did you grow up around here?"

She nodded, "Sure did, and I couldn't imagine living anywhere else. Big cities aren't my thing and I love the lifestyle that Royal has to offer."

"It's a different pace here, that's for sure."

"What about you?" she asked, happy to turn the tables on him for a change. Even though she was fairly certain of the answer, she couldn't help probing. "Girlfriend?"

His face closed again, all warmth replaced by a sorrow that flashed briefly across his face. "No girlfriend," he said emphatically. "Too many other things going on in my life."

And what would they be? Sophie wondered as the

waiter interrupted them to take their orders. After ordering a lamb shank braised in red wine, she wasn't at all surprised to hear Zach order the eye fillet steak. He looked like a man who liked his red meat.

"Lamb?" he said to her after the waiter had taken their orders and moved away from the table. "You come to what is essentially the best steak house in Texas and you order lamb?"

Sophie shrugged. "It's what appealed to me at the time. At least I ordered a domestic wine, not some fancy imported beer. And here I thought you were proudly American all the way?"

"Fair point." Zach nodded slowly, then smiled as said fancy imported beer was put in front of him and her Californian white zinfandel placed before her.

She watched as he took a long pull of the chilled lager, her eyes mesmerized by the muscles working in his throat and then by the smile of satisfaction on his beautiful features as he put the glass back down in front of him. Oh, how she wished that she could be the reason behind a smile like that from him one day. The second the thought formed, she beat it to the back of her mind again. That way could only lead to trouble.

"Now that makes a hard day at the office worthwhile," he said with a soul-deep gratification that brought another smile to her face.

"Simple pleasures, huh?"

He looked at her as if to check if she was still teasing him after the imported beer comment, then gave another nod of acknowledgment. "Yeah, when it comes down to it, it's the simple things that matter the most. Don't you agree?"

"Totally. For me it's home and family. One day I hope to have both."

"You've made a lovely home out of your apartment."

"Thank you, but it's still not mine, y'know? Soon I hope to be able to put a deposit on a place of my own. Something small, with a bit of a garden. Somewhere that I can truly call mine."

And that was another reason why she was so darned worried about Alex Santiago. What if he didn't come back? Would Zach continue to keep the business running or would he fold things up and go back to where he'd come from? Where would she be then? She earned good money now and her options within Royal to earn the same weren't bountiful. If she lost her job, that could be the end of her dream of owning her own home—she'd never earn enough to make mortgage payments and to afford extras like the private investigator she'd hired to find her sister.

"And that's important to you because?" Zach coaxed.

She took a moment to think before answering. "Stability, not being at someone else's whim or mercy."

"Sounds like there's some history there."

She shrugged. "Isn't there always?"

"Can you tell me?"

Sophie sighed. It wasn't something she tended to bandy about, but there was something about Zach's gentle questioning that made her actually want to tell him.

"Nothing spectacular. My dad died when I was a baby and my mom remarried. They had my sister and life was great for a while, but then a few years later my new dad died in an accident at work and our lives turned upside down. We had to move out of our home and my sister went to live with her aunt, because Mom couldn't cope with us both with the hours she had to work to make the rent. It was hard for her," Sophie added just in case Zach felt inclined to be judgmental. "We had to keep moving around, which I hated, but even then I used to keep house to help Mom out. She'd usually juggle two jobs, or pull double shifts when she only had one source of income. Things settled down a bit after I finished college. She met someone new, they married and I moved out and got my own place."

"They kicked you out?"

Zach sounded defensive and Sophie rushed to dis-abuse him of that. "No, not at all. But I was ready to stand on my own two feet. Mom and Jim marrying didn't make any difference to that. No, that's not en-tirely true. I felt better about moving to a place of my own, knowing she'd be taken care of."

Zach looked at Sophie across the table. She'd talked more personally to him tonight than she ever had in the time they'd worked together, but there was a huge amount she wasn't saying. Listening to her, he could begin to understand why she was so good at what she did. She was used to keeping things together, keeping things calm. It was a sure bet that she'd done her best to help her mother out at home from an early age—that ca-pable manner of hers was second nature now, but there had probably been a time when it was all about security.

His own upbringing had been completely the oppo-site. At least up until his dad had been laid off from his job. Even then, forced to take on a menial position at a much lower wage, his father had insisted on paying Zach's way through college. It was one of the reasons Zach worked so hard now. He didn't ever want to be in the position his parents had been when his father's job had been downsized. And he'd made it up to them for all the sacrifices they'd made to ensure he'd had the best opportunities available to him. It didn't sound like Sophie had been so lucky.

"And your sister? She's the one in that photo you had with you on Monday, right?"

Sophie inclined her head, her cap of hair swinging gently forward to caress her cheek. His fingers itched to do the same and he reached for the dewy glass in front of him instead.

"You said you don't stay in touch. How come?"

"Her aunt formally adopted her several months after she took Suzie to live with them. She told Mom they didn't think it was good for Suzie to continue to have contact with us. Said it was too disruptive."

There was a world full of hurt and loss in her simply chosen words.

"And your mother agreed to that?" he said incredulously.

Sophie's eyes flamed. "You have no idea of what it was like for my mother. Don't you dare judge her."

Zach put up both hands in surrender. "Whoa, I'm sorry. I didn't mean to touch a nerve there."

After Anna's car wreck, he'd fought tooth and nail to keep his son—arguing with doctors and specialists until he was blue in the face. But after Blake had been on life support for six weeks and the doctors had repeatedly told him his son had no brain activity, Zach and Anna had had to let him go. For the life of him he couldn't understand how a parent could give up a child the way Sophie's mother had, not when she had every reason to fight to keep her.

"Mom couldn't work and take care of us both at the same time. I was in school. Mom couldn't afford day care and Suzie, well, she was a bit of a handful. She had been a demanding baby and that didn't change as she got older. She was always just that bit more vulnerable than I was, needed that much more attention. Giving Suzie up wasn't Mom's first choice, not by any means, but she had to do what was best—for all of us. And Suzie's aunt, well, family money aside, her late husband had been a very wealthy man. She didn't have to work and she was childless. Mom knew that Suzie would be the center of her world, that she'd be loved and cared for as she deserved to be—in ways we couldn't."

Her choice of words—saying "we" rather than "she"—explained so much about the person she was today. He didn't doubt that Sophie harbored some guilt that she hadn't been able to look after her sister enough or to help her mother more so that their small family wouldn't have to be broken up. He tried to imagine what it would be like growing up feeling like that, and couldn't.

"Sophie," he said reaching across the small table to take her trembling hand in his, "I'm sorry. I didn't mean to sound judgmental. It must have been tough."

She hesitated a moment and he could feel her inner battle rage as she fought to drag her emotions back under control. Eventually she pulled her hand out from beneath his.

"It was, but it's in the past now."

But it wasn't in the past. He could see that just by looking at her. The hurts, the loss—they were all still there. Their shadows lingered beneath the calm surface she presented to the rest of the world.

Zach fought the nearly overwhelming urge he had to tell her it would be all right, that he would do what he could to assuage the pain of her past, that he'd fight her dragons for her and lay them at her feet. Grappling to get his own emotions under control, he reminded himself that he'd already taken that road once before, with Anna, and look where that had led them. No, the last thing he needed was to complicate his life with another wounded bird.

He all but welcomed the waiter out loud when the man arrived with their plates of steaming-hot food, and Zach turned the conversation to more general things, including the latest developments at the Texas Cattleman's Club. He entertained Sophie with a passable impersonation of Beau Hacket's blustering about the new child-care center. By the time they'd finished their meal and enjoyed dessert and coffee, he thought he'd managed to chase those shadows from her eyes. Even if only for an evening.

He wished he had a reason to make their night last longer. She was good company and, when the conversation stayed well and truly off the personal, a great talker. Even more, she was a perceptive listener—he supposed that was part of why she was so darn good at her job. She was always subconsciously taking note of what was happening around her, always ready to put her hand on what was needed almost before the need arose.

Sophie Beldon appealed to him on an intellectual level, and her subtle beauty was a siren call—from the way her eyes began to sparkle before she would laugh right down to the enticing shadow of her breasts at the V of her neckline. And her mouth. God, her mouth. A jolt of longing shook him to his core. What would it be like to taste her, to feel the softness of those lips against his, to command their surrender?

Zach placed his coffee cup back on its saucer none too gently, a tremor in his hand betraying the need that fought for dominance over his heretofore steely control. Control won in the end as he signaled to the waiter for their check. He slid his card in the wallet and when the waiter returned with the receipt, he signed off with a generous tip.

He had to get Sophie home before he did or said something stupid. Before he went over the invisible line he'd drawn in respect of his working relationship, and *only* his working relationship, with her.

They made small talk on the short journey to her apartment building, extolling the virtues of the chef at Claire's and how much they'd enjoyed the food. When they pulled up outside her ground-floor unit, it was second nature to Zach to get out of the car first and open her door for her. He walked her up the short path and waited while she extracted her key from her bag.

"Well, thank you for a lovely meal. I really enjoyed it," she said simply once the key was in her hand.

Before he could reply, she stepped in closer and leaned up to place a kiss on his cheek. That was all it took for his instincts to kick in, for him to turn his face so that her lips met his instead. His arm curled around her waist to draw her more closely against his body and he angled his head ever so slightly so he could deepen their kiss.

Heat sizzled along his veins. Her lips were every bit as soft and delicious as he'd imagined and the tiny sound she made in the back of her throat sent his pulse racing. This was way more than he'd imagined—this scorching desire combined with the raging need he'd managed to keep firmly under control for so very long. Emotion rocked him, sharp and intense, and he knew their working relationship could never be the same again. He wanted Sophie Beldon from the gleaming top of her blond head to the tips of her dainty feet and everything, yes, definitely everything in between.

His hips flexed lightly against the softness of her belly. Her answering press back against him reminded him of what it felt like to be a man—to want with a gut-aching need so strong that it almost hurt to desire another human being this much.

And then, just like that, it was over. Cool night air swirled in the space between them. She was pulling away, her eyes glittering like whiskey-colored topaz, her lips still moist from their kiss and slightly swollen with the evidence of their all-too-brief passion. She dipped her head in that way she had, closing her eyes briefly.

"Don't," he said sharply.

"Don't?"

"Don't hide from me. From us."

"There is no us, is there?" she asked, her voice slightly shaky.

Every cell in his body urged him to say, "Yes, there is an us." To take her back into his arms again and to repeat the intimacy of what they'd just shared. But reason intruded with harsh reality. They worked together. More than that, they had to hold things together in the office until Alex's absence could be explained and he, hopefully, returned. And then there was Anna. The reminder was as sobering as an icy-cold shower.

"No, you're right. I'll see you Monday?" he said, stepping back from her—away from temptation.

"Yes, Monday."

He waited by his car until she let herself inside her apartment, and watched as her outside light went out, followed by the living room lights being turned on. Even then he had to force himself to get in his car and to start it up, put it in gear and drive away. He was a fool. He should never have let things get away like that. Never. It went against his code of ethics in so many ways, and yet there was still this invisible thread that pulled between them. A thread that grew tighter with the more distance he put between them.

Five

"*You kissed him!*"

"Mia, please, shh!" Sophie hissed across the table of the booth she shared with her friend Mia Hughes. "Besides, it was only supposed to be a short peck, a good-night and thank-you, not…not what it turned into, that's for sure."

Her nerve endings still buzzed with excitement even now, fourteen hours since Zach had seen her to her door. Fourteen hours since she'd been introduced to the most searing, blistering ardor she'd ever experienced in her entire twenty-eight years.

Mia moved in closer. "So, tell me. Did he make your toes curl?"

"Oh, Lord, yes. And everything in between."

"I knew it!" Mia laughed, leaning back against the back of the banquette. "Beneath that *GQ* look, he definitely has that smoldering-hot thing going on. Plus, he's so dark and mysterious."

Sophie squirmed in her seat and almost immediately wished she hadn't. Her body still hummed from the aftereffects of their kiss and the action just seemed to increase her discomfort.

"I still don't know what possessed me to do it," she confided in her friend.

"I know," Mia said confidently. "You've been attracted to him for the longest time. It was the next natural step."

"Well, natural or not, it isn't happening again. I kind of put him off."

"You what?"

Mia's voice rose again, attracting the attention of the other patrons of the Royal Diner. Sophie felt her cheeks flame.

"Do you think you could maybe keep it down a bit?" she pleaded with her friend.

Mia looked like she was all control—her long dark-brown hair wound into a tight knot at the back of her head, her complexion flawless, the makeup around her bright-blue eyes subtle yet still managing to emphasize her natural beauty. She was usually quiet and no-nonsense, so her outburst surprised them both.

"I'm sorry," Mia said, contrite. "It's just you surprised me. You've been hungering for this guy for the longest time and you're telling me *you* were the one to back off?"

"It was too much."

"What, exactly, was too much?"

"Don't you put your counselor face on with me," Sophie laughed.

"Hey, I haven't finished my degree yet," Mia reminded her. "And don't try to distract me."

Sophie sighed. "Everything. Being with him for a

meal out, kissing him good night." She rubbed her eyes with the fingers of her right hand. "Even when he arrived and I had to get him to help me do up my dress."

Mia's face said everything her mouth didn't.

"Yeah, I got my zipper stuck just before he arrived. I couldn't get it loose and I had to ask Zach for help. He... he touched me. It was totally accidental and it was only with the backs of his fingers, but all evening I couldn't help but wonder—if I felt like that at a slight touch, what would it be like to have him really touch me?"

"You got it bad, girl," her friend teased.

"I know. If I'm not careful I'll ruin everything. We have to work together, for goodness' sake."

Mia smiled. "No reason why you can't have work and a bit of play."

"I dunno." Sophie shook her head. "I keep feeling like there's something going on with him. Something that he's trying to keep quiet. What if it's to do with Alex's disappearance?"

Mia was employed as Alex's housekeeper at his mansion in Pine Valley—it was a personal arrangement that Alex handled himself and fell outside of Sophie's responsibilities in the office. The hours were perfect for her while she finished up her counseling degree, and Sophie knew for herself what a generous boss Alex was. The work had never been terribly demanding, but with Alex missing Mia had become more of a well-paid house sitter than housekeeper. Sophie's words brought a frown to Mia's brow.

"You really think he might be involved?"

Sophie shrugged. "I don't want to think he is, but he's working strange hours lately and he's kind of secretive, y'know? Like putting people on hold if I come into his office while he's on the phone, or closing his laptop so I can't see the screen. It's not like him. I mean, sure, he's not exactly an open book on any day of the week, but he's even more closed than usual. And even last night he kept turning the conversation to me every time I tried to learn a bit more about him. He said he wanted us to be friends."

"Friends?"

"Yeah, and in my book, friendship is a two-way street."

"Hmm," Mia answered, looking thoughtful.

"What are you thinking about?"

"Well, of anyone, you're probably in the best position to figure out what he's up to, wouldn't you say?"

"Except I don't know what he's up to, that's the problem. It's not as if I haven't tried, but he's always a step ahead of me."

"Maybe you need to investigate a bit more. Check his computer? Check his phone log? Alex has to be somewhere. No one just disappears into thin air. He could even have planned this all along and Zach could have helped him. We can't automatically assume that Zach could be a bad guy in this."

"You're right," Sophie agreed slowly. "He might be helping Alex. I sure hope if he is involved, it's for that reason and not for anything sinister."

"I don't think he's involved in anything bad. If anyone is, it'd be that rat-bag David Firestone. Before Alex went missing, he asked me to make sure he had some champagne on ice. When I asked him what he was celebrating, he told me he'd beaten Firestone on an investment property deal. Apparently Firestone wasn't very happy when Alex beat him to the punch."

"Do you think Firestone could have done something to Alex? Was he really that angry?" Sophie asked.

"From what I understand, he was pretty steamed up. And I dunno, but he looks to me like the kind of guy who'd exact revenge if he thought it was due." Mia lifted her coffee cup and took a sip, then shuddered. "Cold, yuck!"

"I wonder where Alex is," Sophie mused.

"Yeah. I still can't help thinking that something bad has happened to him. He took nothing from the house. Not a change of clothes, nothing."

Sophie pushed away her plate, half her lunch still uneaten. "What can we do?"

"Information. We can gather information. It's the only thing we can do. You need to find out whatever you can from Zach if he knows more than he's letting on and I'll do what I can from Alex's side of things, especially about what he might have known about David Firestone. There has to be something at the house that can point us in the right direction." Mia leaned forward and reached for Sophie's hand. "By the way, speaking of information. How is it going with the investigator you hired to find your sister? Any luck?"

Sophie shook her head. "No. We thought he had a lead earlier in the week but it turned out to be another dead end." She met her friend's compassionate gaze. "What if it's all a waste of time, Mia? What if she's dead?"

"Wouldn't you rather know?" her friend said softly, giving her hand a reassuring squeeze.

"I guess so, and something tells me she's still out there."

"Then trust that feeling to bring her home." Mia cast a glance at her watch. "Speaking of home, I'd better head back to Pine Valley."

"How are things there? Are the media still camping out at the gates?"

Mia pulled a face. "They are. It's getting so bad I almost pulled out of coming today. I'm worried sick someone will break into the property and start poking around."

"But the police already went through the house, didn't they? If they couldn't find anything to explain where Alex might have gone, then I doubt any journalists could, either."

"Try telling them that," Mia answered with a wry grin. "Anyway, I'd better get going, I still have some studying to do. My turn to treat for lunch, okay?"

"That makes it my turn to tip," Sophie answered, leaving a few bills on the table.

The two women took turns to pay for lunch, even though Sophie would have been more than happy to have treated Mia more often. She knew her friend had tuition due soon, and while Alex was a generous boss, Sophie doubted that Mia could afford to splurge too frequently.

But at the cash register, both women were surprised when Mia's card was declined.

"Don't worry, I'll cover it." Sophie rapidly stepped up and unfolded the necessary bills.

"I don't understand it," Mia said, her face a little paler than usual and a worried frown creasing her brow.

"It'll just be some glitch at the bank. Give them a call and I'm sure you'll have it sorted out in no time. Look, can I loan you some money to tide you over the weekend? At least until you can sort things out with the bank?"

"No, no. I'll be fine. I'm sure."

Mia unlocked her car and threw her friend a quick

smile, but Sophie could tell she wasn't mollified. She didn't want to push. Mia was nothing if not proud and guarded her independence carefully.

"Well, don't hesitate to ask if I can do anything for you, okay? I mean it, Mia."

It was all she could do under the circumstances.

"Sure," Mia answered although Sophie knew her friend would rather walk through a field filled with ornery rodeo bulls than ask for help.

"Oh, and be careful about that guy, Firestone."

"I will, don't you worry," Mia said with a smile and a cheeky wink. "And don't do anything with your Mr. Lassiter that I wouldn't do."

Sophie couldn't help it. She blushed red hot again. She opened her car and settled inside, accompanied by the ring of Mia's laughter at her reaction. As she drove back home, she wondered just how far she'd be prepared to go to elicit information from Zach.

"Don't be ridiculous," she growled at her reflection in the rearview mirror. "You're no Mata Hari."

No, she definitely wasn't, but it didn't stop a ripple of anticipation from undulating from her core to her extremities. Could she do it? Could she try to seduce the information out of him? It went against everything she had inside of her and even if he did prove willing, there was nothing to say that he was the kind of guy who'd divulge his secrets during a bit of pillow talk.

Her inner muscles clenched tight at the thought of what it would take to actually lead to said pillow talk. She weighed it in her head during the journey home and all through her afternoon tidying around her home and getting her laundry done—her work outfits all pressed and ready for the week ahead. By the time she donned her nightgown and tucked herself into fresh, clean sheets, together with the latest novel she'd picked up, she was still a bundle of nervous energy and sick to death of the inner battle she'd waged with herself.

"Toss a coin," she said out loud when she couldn't settle into reading her book.

Sophie pushed back her covers and rose from the bed to cross the room and take her coin purse from her handbag. She grabbed a nickel and studied it carefully for a full minute before placing it on her thumbnail, ready to flick it into the air.

"Heads, I do it. Tails, I don't," she muttered grimly.

She flicked. The coin executed a graceful arc before she grabbed it with one hand, laying it flat on the back of the other with her fingers still covering what decision it had made. Slowly, she lifted her fingers.

Heads.

Six

"Best of three," she said on a whoosh of air.

Heads.

Heads.

Somewhere out there, someone had to be laughing at her, Sophie decided before returning the coin to her purse and climbing back between the sheets.

So the fates had decided she was to seduce whatever information she could out of Zach regarding his knowledge, or otherwise, of Alex's disappearance. Sounded simple, really. She flopped back against her perfectly aligned feather pillows and huffed out a sigh. She'd never succeed. She'd been the one to stop things going any further when he'd kissed her good night.

Then, surely, she had the right to change her mind…

Sophie reached out to flick off her bedside light and lay in the darkness staring blindly toward her ceiling. This was big. More than big, it was monumental. It went against everything she'd ever been brought up to be. But she owed it to Alex, didn't she? Her boss deserved someone in his corner. Oh, sure, she knew the police were investigating, but so far they'd been unable to turn up any solid leads. What if Zach had been actively pushing them in the wrong direction?

She rolled onto her side and closed her eyes. What if he hadn't? What if her conjecture was nothing but smoke and mirrors? At worst she'd potentially embarrass herself horribly, and she cringed at the thought. But at best, well, at best she could possibly find out vital information about Alex while in all likelihood having the very best sex of her life. And if this crazy scheme of hers turned out to be completely off the mark, well, it wasn't as if she wasn't powerfully attracted to Zach or that interest wasn't reciprocated. Who knew where things could lead?

A groan ripped from her throat and she threw herself onto her other side in disgust. It all sounded so mercenary. She was nothing like the kind of person who could carry this off. She wasn't designed for intrigue and seduction. She liked order, security. But that very security was threatened if she lost her job. While Alex and Zach were business partners, Zach could just as easily conduct his business anywhere but Royal. There was nothing and no one to hold him here.

She tried to think it all through logically, to weigh the pros against the cons, but as sleep claimed her she was no closer to a resolution. The next morning, after a surprisingly restful sleep, Sophie woke with the answer clear in her mind. Zach had already shown he was attracted to her, but he'd respected her when she'd stepped back. She'd leave it to him to make her decision for her. But nothing said she couldn't try to sway that decision in her favor.

She crossed the room to her wardrobe and considered the five outfits she'd hung in order for her Monday to Friday office wear. No, these wouldn't do at all. Not in their current incarnations, anyway. Sophie unhooked the suit and camisole that she'd decided on for Monday and tossed the camisole onto her bed. Was the neckline of the suit too bold or, with the right bra, would it be perfect for Operation: Seduction?

She giggled to herself as she put the suit back on the rail and considered Tuesday's ensemble. Yes, this could work, too. Instead of buttoning the form-fitting blouse to her throat, she could easily flick a few extra buttons open, and maybe wear a pendant—she had exactly the right one in her jewelry box—that would draw the eye, specifically Zach's eye, down.

Was he a boob man or a leg man, she wondered. No harm in covering all bases, she decided, eschewing Wednesday's getup as way too staid for the new Sophie Beldon. Instead, she reached for a short, straight skirt she saved for nights out with her girlfriends. Even her legs, which she'd always considered too short to be beautiful, looked good in this. Stacked with a set of heels she'd be invincible.

Sophie laughed out loud. She was starting to enjoy this.

"Roll on Monday," she said to herself as she closed her wardrobe and went to get herself some breakfast. "I can't wait."

Zach felt every one of his thirty-four years come Monday morning. Over the weekend he'd spent time on a video conference with a panel of doctors at the private mental health clinic he wanted to admit Anna to. Problem was, she'd dropped off the radar. Her parents said they hadn't heard from her over the weekend, something that wasn't unusual in their experience but, for Zach, combined with Anna's ultrafragile state of mind, it was red flag of titanic proportions.

When he hadn't been able to reach Anna on her mobile phone all day Saturday, he'd driven the fifty miles to Midland on Sunday morning. But the house they'd previously shared had been empty, without even a sign of recent occupation. It had all but slaughtered him to go upstairs to check the bedrooms and to discover that even now, almost two years since Blake's death, his nursery was still in the same state of casual disarray as it had been on the day Anna had taken him in the car and driven away after yet another argument with Zach.

None of her friends seemed to know where she was and it frustrated the hell out of him that he seemed to be the only person truly concerned about her whereabouts. If she'd ended up hurting herself, or worse, he didn't know if he would ever be able to forgive himself for not acting sooner to keep her safe.

Compounding his concern for his ex-wife was the complication of how he felt about Sophie Beldon. Taking her out on Friday night had seemed like a good idea at the time, but after a chillingly cold shower when he'd arrived home, he'd begun to examine his sanity in pursuing her as he had, even if it was as subtle as turning a chaste good night peck on the cheek to something so much more. He could have sworn the air around them had crackled with the energy that sprang to life between them. But she'd pulled back, and he'd been gentlemanly enough not to attempt to override her decision, no matter how much his libido had screamed at him to do otherwise.

Zach pushed open the door to the executive suite and started toward his office, only to be halted by Sophie coming out of the kitchenette.

"Ah, there you are. Good morning. Would you like coffee?"

He stopped in his tracks, his eyes locked on her as if seeing her for the first time, his mouth suddenly dry. Words failed him. He'd seen her wear this suit before, several times in fact. But he'd never seen her wear it quite like this. The rich amber fabric was a perfect foil for her eyes and the shining cap of her blond hair, but it wasn't the color that had arrested him. No, it was the fact that she most definitely wasn't wearing her usual demure something underneath it. And her breasts, they were soft gentle mounds peaking up against the lapels of her jacket.

"Zach? Coffee?" she prompted with a sweet smile.

"Uh, yeah. Coffee. Thanks. That'd be great."

He forced himself to turn toward his office and get himself under control. He felt as if he'd been ambushed and shook his head slightly. No. He had to be imagining things. And he continued to console himself with that thought right up until she came into his office with a steaming mug of coffee and bent down to place it on his desk.

Oh, yes, definitely ambushed. A hint of white musk and vanilla and something else that made him want to reach for her and repeat their embrace of Friday night— and more. Worse, though, was the glimpse he got of soft, warm flesh encased in some frothy cream-colored lingerie.

"Thanks," he said through gritted teeth. "Any news from the sheriff this morning?"

Sophie straightened and made a little moue with her lips. Darn it all. What was it with him and her lips?

"Nothing yet," she said. "Is there anything in particular you need me for today?"

He could think of several things right off the top of his head. None of them had anything to do with the work at hand, however.

"I'm fine," he said, reaching for the coffee and taking a long sip of the brew, burning his tongue and the roof of his mouth in the process.

He welcomed the pain; it was the perfect distraction from the torture his body was going through.

"Okay, then. Well, if you need me, you know where to find me."

She exited his office and he couldn't tear his eyes off her. It wasn't just his imagination. She was different from last week. Way different, and yet no less appealing.

And so it went each day. Her new fragrance, while subtle, managed to stay with him every hour in the office, driving him crazy. He was on edge constantly, and in a state of semiarousal from the instant he set foot in the executive suite until he drove himself back to his empty mansion containing his all-too-empty bed each night.

But it was her subtle brushes against his body when he least expected it that were his undoing. They were working late on Thursday night and she'd brought him the reports he'd been waiting on so he could send them out to investors with his recommendation. She brushed lightly past him as he stood staring at the mounting piles of paper on his desk, the outside edge of her breast touching ever so slightly against his shoulder.

The heat of her body seared through the blue silk blouse she wore and transferred past the high-quality cotton of his tailor-made shirt with the conductivity of electricity.

"Sorry," he said, pulling away from her even though it was her contact.

"No problem. Will that be all tonight?" she asked, barely moving a scant inch from his side.

"Yeah, you can go. Thanks for staying with me."

"No problem. What about you? Are you heading home now?"

"No, I still want to give these a final pass-through and compose the individual letters."

She turned slightly so her cutely shaped backside was resting against the edge of his desk.

"You're working too hard, Zach. Don't you think you should lighten up, loosen that tie of yours a little and cut yourself some slack?"

Slack? There was nothing slack in his body right now, in fact, every working part of him was exactly the opposite—taut and aching and frustratingly unsatisfied. Words failed him as she leaned a little closer.

"Or maybe I should just loosen it for you?"

Her fingers undid the work of his perfect Windsor knot in a matter of seconds, then gently flicked the top button of his shirt undone.

"There, isn't that more comfortable?" she said with a curve of her lips.

Before he knew it his hands were at her wrists, tugging her toward him until they were face-to-face.

"Comfortable? I'll show you comfortable."

He leaned forward and captured her mouth with his.

The relief was instant but short-lived as the perfection of kissing her incited a whole raft of new sensations within him. He pulled away.

"Tell me to stop now and I will," he growled, barely able to hold on to his instincts a moment longer.

In answer, Sophie captured his face between her hands and pulled him back toward her, her tongue slipping between his lips to caress and entice and thoroughly chase away any last rational thought of control. He gave over to the moment, to the rush of desire that consumed his body. For the first time this week, everything felt right. He sank into her warmth, her welcome.

She tasted of coffee and a sweetness that was pure Sophie and he couldn't get enough of her. His hands skimmed up her rib cage to touch the sides of her breasts. She groaned and pressed herself against him, her hands now on the buttons of her blouse, pulling them open and exposing the silver-gray lace cups of her bra. Behind the sheer fabric he could see her nipples, taut and prominent nubs of palest pink.

Zach bent his head to the warm swells of her flesh, pressing his lips to the crevice created by the push-up effect of her bra. Sophie shuddered in his arms as he reached behind her and unsnapped the hooks on her bra, releasing her breasts.

"You're beautiful, so beautiful," he said reverently, palming the full globes, his thumbs brushing over her nipples, drawing them to attention even more.

"You make me feel beautiful," she whispered in return, her hands now busy yanking his tie from his collar and loosening the rest of his buttons.

"I want you, Sophie."

"I want you, too. So much. For so long."

Her words slowly sank in. He'd been holding back,

determined not to engage in a relationship with her and she'd been willing all along? He was a crazy fool. Here she was, as hungry for him as he was for her, and he'd been nobly refusing to follow what his body had been begging for all this time.

Her small hands pushed his shirt aside before spreading across his chest. He gasped at the sensation of her fingers on his skin. It had been so long since he'd allowed himself to give and receive physical affection, to have pleasure from meeting a need that went soul deep.

He kissed her again, and again and again, his mind a haze of need and want and sensation. Somewhere along the line she shed her skirt, revealing tiny panties to match her bra and thigh-high stockings with lacy tops. His fingers skimmed the lace, stroked the softness of her skin, felt her tremble at his touch. His hand worked slowly past the edge of her underwear to the neatly trimmed thatch of hair at the apex of her thighs, his fingers stroking her heated core, feeling her wetness, her desire for him.

He reached behind her to push aside the papers he'd been so fixated on only moments ago and gently coaxed her backward onto the surface of his desk. Her legs splayed over the edge and he felt his breath catch in his throat. He'd never seen anything more wanton, nor more exquisitely feminine in his life. Zach slid his fingers into the sides of her panties, drawing them down her legs, exposing her lush femininity to him. She was spread before him like a feast to be devoured, and he a man who hadn't dined in so long he'd almost forgotten what pleasure was anymore.

Zach stood between her legs and bent over Sophie's prone figure and kissed her again, her hands thrusting in his hair, then down the back of his neck and to his shoulders, her nails digging into him as he trailed one hand up and down her body, taking his time discovering the shape of her, the feel of her skin against his palms.

"You feel so good," he murmured against her lips.

Beneath his mouth he felt her lips pull into an answering smile. "You should feel it from my side," she said teasingly, her voice ending on a gasp, her body going rigid as his hands trailed lower to tease the tops of her thighs.

"How about I feel *in*side," he responded, his voice thick with longing.

He gently parted her moist flesh and felt her tense in anticipation as he stroked the heated entrance to her body.

"You're enjoying this, aren't you?" she said, her voice strangled.

"Oh, yes."

Zach eased one finger inside her, her heat enveloping him and making another part of his body all the more eager to follow in kind. He stroked her inner walls and gently pressed his palm against her clitoris. The instant he did so, it was as if it catalyzed her body into paroxysms of pleasure. Her inner muscles clenched rhythmically around his finger, her hips strained upward and her cry of satisfaction filled the office. He slowed his movements, taking his time, easing his hand free even as she reached for him, dragging his belt undone and unzipping his trousers.

He almost lost it as her hands closed around his straining erection through his boxer briefs, but somehow he managed to regain control.

"I don't have any protection," he said through clenched teeth as she freed him from his underwear and stroked him from base to tip.

"I'm protected," she said in invitation. "Seriously, I'm clean, I have regular checks, I haven't had a partner in at least a year and I'm on the injection."

"Same, except more than two years and while my shots are up-to-date, we're probably not talking about the same thing."

He smiled, caught by the random humor of the situation even as his body trembled and his brain, and other parts of him, demanded he simply take her and be done with it. Take both of them on a ride to deliver a maelstrom of feeling. Sophie stroked his length once more, making him hiss a sharp breath in between his teeth.

"Then what on earth are you waiting for?"

"Are you certain you want this?" he asked, desperately trying to maintain his equilibrium even though he felt as if the top of his head would blow off any second now from the pressure building inside him. "I'm—I... I haven't been with anyone in a long time."

She met his gaze full-on. "I'm certain. I trust you, Zach, and you can trust me, too. I'm not the kind of girl who—"

It was all he needed to hear. "Shh, I know. I trust you."

And with those words of acceptance, he slid inexorably inside her body. Zach dragged in a deep breath and slowly withdrew again. This was pleasure and pain and everything in between. The gratifying impression of her slick body clasped around him, the piercing agony of holding back, of gripping the last vestiges of control. It was too much, especially when Sophie drew her feet up behind him. He heard her shoes drop to the floor seconds before her heels dug into his buttocks.

"Take me, Zach. I'm all yours."

The dam of constraint burst and he surged forward,

again and again until the sensations that drove him spiraled out of control. Vaguely he was aware of Sophie cresting another climax before his own flashed through his body—a kaleidoscope of color and sensuality, of connection and completion, of give and take.

He groaned as he collapsed, none too gently, upon her. Sophie's arms closed tight around his body, holding him as if she'd never let him go. His heartbeat pounded at a mega rate as aftershocks of fulfillment shuddered through him. Finally he pushed himself up, mindful of his weight on Sophie's much smaller frame.

Zach reluctantly withdrew from her body, his own instantly mourning the unforgettably sweet intimacy of their skin-to-skin contact.

"Are you okay?" he asked, extending a hand to her and helping her to her feet.

"Never better," she answered and went up on tiptoes to kiss him.

Despite having enjoyed mind-numbing sex with her only seconds ago, desire slammed into him anew and he wrapped his arms around her slender form and drew her firmly against his body, deepening their embrace. The buzz of his mobile phone caught his attention.

Sophie pulled out of his arms.

"I'll go and tidy myself up while you take that," she said, with another quick buss against his cheek.

He watched as she collected her things, her movements graceful as she walked naked out his office door and toward the private bathrooms that were part of the executive suite. He ached to follow her but his phone continued to buzz insistently.

He swept it up and answered it without checking the caller ID.

"Zach? Is that you?"

Anna.

Guilt slammed into him with the weight of a runaway freight train.

Seven

Guilt laced with a hefty dose of relief. They hadn't been a couple in any sense of the word for years—their marriage broken long before the ink was dry on their divorce papers—but she still needed him and relief won out as he silently thanked God she was okay.

"Yeah, it's me. Where have you been?"

"Oh, just away. I—I needed some space, some time to think about things. The neighbors said you were around, looking for me. Was it something special you needed me for?"

She sounded distant, as if her mind was on something else. Zach's concern inched up a few notches.

"No, nothing special. I just couldn't get hold of you and I was worried about you. Is everything okay?"

"I'm fine, Zach. No need to worry. Everything's just fine."

"Have you been taking your meds?"

"Of course I have. Despite what you may think, I can look after myself."

That was something he very much doubted. And the way she was talking worried him even more. She'd gone from calling him every day, crying through the phone, racked with grief for their dead son, to this. He'd call her parents and see if they could persuade her to stay with them for a few days. At least then he'd be able to relax in the knowledge someone was keeping an eye on her until he could convince her to see the doctors at the clinic.

"Okay," he said, forcing himself to sound calm. "I believe you, Anna. I depend on you to take care of yourself."

"Not to disappoint you, you mean."

He flinched. He didn't deserve that. "You don't disappoint me."

"But I did, didn't I?"

He sighed and closed his eyes. "We've moved past that now."

"Have we?"

"Anna, please. Don't do this to yourself."

"I'm sorry, Zach. Have I told you how sorry I am?"

Her earlier calm gone, her words were threaded with the grief he knew was on the verge of consuming her whole.

"You have, Anna, and it's okay. You have to believe me. It's time to move forward."

"I'm trying, but it's so hard."

"I know," he consoled. And he did know. There wasn't a day that went by that he didn't think about what Blake would have been doing had he lived. "But you're stronger than you think, Anna. You will get through this. Look, why don't you pack a bag? I'll call your parents and get them to take you back to their place for the weekend so you have some company, okay?"

"Okay. Yeah, I'd like that."

Zach quietly sighed and felt his body relax. She would be safe for now, at least. Getting her assurance she would pack her bag right that minute, he ended the call and then dialed his former in-laws, who were only too happy to agree to his suggestion that they take her into their home for a few nights. This disappearance of hers had given them a wake-up call and he could only hope that they'd be on board when he talked to them about Anna entering a professional care facility to guide her out of the black hole her grief had become before it consumed her whole.

Zach disconnected the call with his ex-father-in-law, closed his eyes and hoped with all his heart that Anna would be safe with them. Her parents had brushed off two earlier suicide attempts as accidental overdoses. Of course she hadn't meant to do it, her parents had argued when he'd struggled to make them see she needed more than just their help to get through. Their favored excuse was that she just had trouble sleeping since the accident, the other that she had trouble controlling the pain in her neck that continued to be a reminder of the whiplash she'd sustained in the crash.

He didn't deny that Anna had trouble with both those things, but her problems went far deeper, and since her parents were stubbornly oblivious to them, it was up to him to make sure she found a path out of her darkness. She needed someone in her corner to fight for her—to fight for her life, in fact.

The tension in his shoulders tightened when Zach opened his eyes and saw the chaos that was his desk. The reminder of what had just transpired in his office.

He reached to the floor to pick up his shirt and dragged it over his body. What an evening of contrasts. To peak on such a glorious high, and then descend to an all-too-sobering low.

Zach finished getting dressed and made a vague attempt to straighten his desk before giving up the idea as hopeless. He'd sort it out in the morning when everything was clearer. He slotted his laptop in its case and, stuffing his tie in his pocket, grabbed his jacket in the other hand and walked out into the reception area of the executive suite.

Sophie stood at her desk. She started to walk toward him, but then hesitated. Uncertainty was clear on her face.

"Are you okay?" she asked, her voice tentative, as if she wasn't sure if she should say anything to him.

Need filled him at the sight and sound of her. Not sexual, just the pure and physical need of one person desperately craving solace from another. He put his things on her desk and opened his arms to her, closing them around her slender form and feeling a deep sense of relief as hers closed around him in return. They stood like that for several minutes, not saying anything, just being—together. It gave him the strength he needed, for now.

Confusion chased through Sophie's mind. When she'd left Zach's office he'd been happy, satisfied. So who had been on the phone and what had they said or done to reduce him to this somber creature in her arms? She held on to him tightly, as if somehow she could infuse her spirit into him—give him the comfort he silently requested and so obviously sought from her.

That he'd come to her and that she could give it to

him made her heart swell with emotion. That he needed it, however, made that knowledge a bittersweet one.

She stroked her hands up and down the long muscles that bordered his spine, relishing the heat and strength of him through the fine cotton of his shirt, and felt him relax in increments. Sophie breathed his scent, like a spray of sea air, crisp and fresh. She'd never be able to visit a beach again, smell the tang of the ocean, without thinking of Zach Lassiter and this moment.

Beneath her cheek on his chest she felt him inhale deeply and then slowly let it go.

"Thank you," he said, loosening his embrace. "I needed that."

"Tough call?" she asked, burning with curiosity yet not knowing exactly how to inquire as to whom he'd spoken to.

His eyes dulled a little and his lips firmed into a straight line before he gave a small nod. "Yeah, but it's okay for now. I'm sorry it had to inter—"

Sophie laid a finger on his lips. "No, don't. Life intrudes. I accept that."

It intruded all too often and too harshly in her experience, which was why she was going to grab this time with him with both hands and hold on with all her might. Her discussions with Mia about seducing information out of Zach paled into insignificance in view of what they'd done here today. The chemistry they shared was all too rare and she knew she wanted more. More of him.

She looked him square in the eyes. "I never thought I'd ever say this to a guy, but here goes. Your place or mine?"

Zach didn't hesitate. "Mine," he said firmly and linked his fingers through hers. "We can stop by your place in the morning for a change of clothes, but up until about then I don't think you're going to need anything else."

Sophie smiled back at him, squeezing his fingers tight. She didn't trust herself to speak, her body racked by a surge of desire so sharp and so extreme it literally made her feel weak in the knees. They moved swiftly through the outer office. She was relieved that the hour was late and the space was empty of their receptionist and handful of admin and accounting staff because she was sure she glowed brightly with what they'd just shared—and what they were about to.

The drive to his home took about thirty minutes and it felt like the longest drive of her life. Every nerve in her body, every cell quivered on high alert. She tried to keep a grip on her thoughts and feelings but everything seemed determined to run through her entire being at Mach speed.

She'd never done anything like she'd done this night—ever. She'd never been the one to take control. Her relationships had always been so organized, for want of a better word. Courtships had followed a set procedure and sex, if it had progressed that far, had been satisfactory. Certainly not the mind-shattering culmination of pleasure she'd experienced tonight beneath Zach's ministrations.

A quiver ran through her at the thought of spending a whole night with him. It had taken every ounce of courage for her to say what she had and she'd fully expected him to bow out, to be polite but firm and excuse himself on one pretext or another. But he hadn't. A tiny inner voice squeed in delight at the prospect of enjoying more of what they'd already shared, of learn-

ing more about what pleased him as well as how he
could please her.

Her stomach tied in a knot of anticipation as Zach
slowed down the SUV he obviously used as his "non-
fun" car and pressed a remote, causing the tall iron gates
in front of them to swing slowly open. He accelerated
up the long driveway and into a large circle, coming
to a halt in front of an imposing two-story mansion
sprawled at the end of the driveway. Subtle exterior
lighting shone on the perfectly manicured lawns and
hedges and trees that had been trimmed and topiaried
within an inch of their lives.

Everything about the exterior screamed money and
for a moment Sophie wondered if she was doing the
right thing. Zach belonged to an entirely different world
than her own. He had money. Real money, and lots of it.

"Are you coming?" Zach asked as he flung open his
door and started to get out.

Sophie nodded and undid her seat belt. By the time
she'd picked her bag up from the car floor, Zach was at
her door and holding it open for her. His manners never
failed to charm her and she unhesitatingly put her hand
in his outstretched one. The instant she did so she was
assailed by desire for Zach—raw, potent, demanding.

She was all but oblivious to moving past the pillared
entryway and over the acres of cream and gold Italian
tile. She automatically placed one foot after the other
up the sweeping carpeted staircase—one hand resting
lightly on the ornately turned black iron railing, the
other still clasped firmly in Zach's heated grip. They
traversed a gallery and stopped momentarily at a set of
double wooden doors.

Zach twisted the handle and thrust the doors open,
pulling Sophie along behind him as he entered the room.

Then all haste ended as he turned to close the doors behind him again. Elegant twin alabaster lamps cast a warm glow over the room from either side of the bed, but Sophie wasn't interested in the rich furnishings or the mile-wide bed on its slightly raised pedestal. She only had eyes for the man standing before her with longing on his face and a promise of more exquisite pleasure in his eyes.

And she wasn't disappointed. While their first coupling had been all haste and achieving satisfaction as quickly as humanly possible, this time they took their time. Learning one another's bodies, discovering the secret places that could reduce them to a quivering mass of need or laughing out loud. And this time when they came together it was slow, languorous and so very, very good.

As Sophie drifted off to sleep in Zach's arms, she knew she'd done the right thing, for both of them. The simmering tension between them had to let go somewhere. How much better was it to have simply given in to the attraction between them? There were no words to describe the drowsy contentment that suffused her—all she knew was that this was way, way more than a crush. She had feelings for Zach Lassiter that went beyond the magnetism that had drawn them together tonight.

Feelings that made her want to chase the shadows from his eyes, to see only joy and laughter reflected there. Feelings that made her wish tonight could be the first of many such nights—for the rest of her life, and his.

Eight

Zach knew the exact moment Sophie drifted off to sleep by the way her body relaxed and grew heavy against him. He pressed his lips to the top of her head, silently wishing her sweet dreams.

Although he was physically shattered, his mind was racing. What had he done? His life was complicated enough already without dragging Sophie into the mix. He should have exhibited some of the restraint Alex had always teased him about—sealed himself behind his so-called ice-man exterior and kept Sophie at bay.

Until last weekend's dinner, he'd had no real clue about how she felt about him. She'd always been warm and friendly, efficient and accommodating. But their kiss that night and her behavior since had steadily chipped through his resolve.

He inhaled the scent of her hair mixed with the fragrance she'd worn recently. Together, they were a heady blend and he could feel his body stir in response. Feel the tendrils of heat curl through him, inch by inch.

No one had ever made him feel like this. He'd never *wanted* anyone with quite this unadulterated desperation. He wanted more, he wanted to explore whether they could actually enjoy a relationship together. Learn all there was to know about one another. They already had the physical harmony down pat. There had been none of the awkwardness of discovering what worked or didn't. Every stroke had been sure, every touch adept. And the way he felt when he entered her body—it was the most sublime experience he'd ever enjoyed. If they could achieve the same synchronicity and understanding mentally, theirs would be a relationship without comparison.

A stab of guilt hit him fair and square in the chest. With Anna in such a vulnerable position, could he allow himself the indulgence of thinking like this, of feeling this way about another woman? What would it do to her? He didn't want to begin to think of how she might react. She depended on him emotionally, so much. It was a burden he'd taken without question. He owed it to her. After all, he should never have bowed to her father's pressure to marry her. He'd been ambitious and stupid, losing sight of his long-term goals and believing that he could shortcut the steps he himself had laid out for his future. Anna had been innocent in all of that.

He was doing his best for her now. Short of actually staying with her and physically taking care of her, which she'd made perfectly clear to him several occasions that she did not want, he'd done the next best thing in sending her home to her mom and dad.

How would she cope, he wondered, if she heard he was in a new relationship? Zach tightened his hold on

Sophie's sleeping form and relished the warmth and feel of her against his naked body. He had barely dated since he and Anna had divorced. He certainly hadn't entered into any intimacy with anyone else—until now. Since she'd fielded the occasional call at the office, Sophie had some idea of Anna's dependency on him. How would she feel, he wondered, about his ex-wife's strong presence in his life? While he was concerned that finding out he had a new woman in his life could be the proverbial straw that broke the camel's back in Anna's case, would Anna be that for Sophie in return?

He clenched his eyes shut. Life could be so complicated. He'd thought he'd had it all under control when he was younger. What a stupid, arrogant fool he'd been to think he could merely follow a plan. People couldn't be categorized so easily, lives couldn't be forced to conform to his expectations. If he'd learned anything from his marriage to Anna, it had been how to adapt to change.

So what about the current change in his life now? Could he embark on what was a potentially precarious office romance, at a time when the office was already in a state of flux? Had the instability of having his business partner missing driven the two of them together and artificially accelerated their feelings for one another? Zach turned the thoughts over and over in his head.

He buried his face in the curve of Sophie's neck, inhaled the scent of her skin and her hair and felt the tension that had been coiling tight inside of him begin to unwind. Even while she was asleep, she did that for him. Soothed him. Eased his worries. And didn't he deserve that? Didn't he deserve some happiness? Some respite from his responsibilities? Sophie brought him that, and more. A decision settled over him before he even realized it. He was going to take what was his to take and let their affair lead where it may. He owed it to himself and he owed it to Sophie.

His body began to relax and he finally allowed sleep to claim him, secure in the knowledge that he could cope with this—one step at a time.

They were running late when they finally hit the office the next morning. A couple of times during the night they'd stirred, reaching for one another in the plush darkness of Zach's master suite to rediscover the highs they could share together. By the time dawn broke, Sophie felt both well used and completely sated. After breakfast in his gourmet kitchen, which had had her itching to inspect the contents of the refrigerator and try out the appliances with some of her favorite recipes, they'd made it to her house in time for her to shower and change into fresh work clothes, applying her makeup even as they drove to work.

Aside from a few raised eyebrows as they entered the building together—Sophie's cheeks flushed and eyes bright from the kiss Zach had planted on her in the elevator—no one had said anything. In fact, it seemed as if today was business as usual, with the exception that her body still hummed with contentment even though she had the odd twinge here and there to remind her of muscles she hadn't used in a while.

She hugged her arms around herself tightly for just a moment and let loose with a grin that spread from ear to ear.

"You look happy," Zach said from behind her. His hand pushed away a swath of her hair, exposing her neck, where he placed a hot, wet kiss just behind her ear. "I have a bone to pick with you."

"Really?" she said, fighting to control the shiver of longing that swept her body at his touch.

"I'm finding it incredibly difficult to focus on the work on my desk today."

Sophie swallowed. She could quite imagine. She got tingles every time she had looked toward his office door this morning.

Zach continued. "Do you have plans for tomorrow night?"

"Me? No, why?"

"The welcome party at the TCC is tomorrow evening, now that my application for membership has been approved. Would you like to come?"

He cast the invitation her way very casually, but she knew what a big deal this was. It was Royal's mark of acceptance from the very elite—the people to whom he looked for business, the people he asked to trust him with their financial stability. No small ask in these turbulent times.

"I'd be honored to attend with you. These events are usually quite formal, aren't they?"

"Yeah, I think so."

"Then I'll make sure I do you proud." She hesitated a moment, seeing a small frown crease his forehead, seeing his eyes look just that little bit distant. "You're thinking about Alex, aren't you?"

"Yeah. It'll be strange accepting the membership offer without my sponsor there. It won't be the same without Alex."

Sophie studied his face carefully, confused by her conflicting thoughts. If Zach truly did have something to do with Alex's disappearance, would he look so genuinely sorry that his friend couldn't be there with him to share the occasion of his entrée into Royal society? Or was he simply a very good actor?

If that was the case, what did that make her? All kidding aside, when she'd decided to investigate whether Zach had anything to do with Alex going missing— at any cost—had she really considered the emotional cost of entering into a physical relationship with him? She'd been stupidly naive not to realize that her heart was already intrinsically wound up in this man. Knowing she was falling for him, could she honestly believe that he was involved?

"Hey," Zach said, tipping her chin up with his knuckle. "I didn't mean to bring you down."

"It's okay. I can only imagine how tough it'll be for you tomorrow."

"I'm glad you'll be there with me," he said simply and the words hit her like blows to her gut.

The laughter she and Mia had shared over Operation: Seduction was a far cry from this reality. From the obvious pain Zach was feeling. There were probably a million reasons why he'd been more reserved than usual recently, why he was spending so much time on the telephone behind a closed office door. Lost for words, she could only give Zach a smile in return.

Work was busy and Zach was out most of the rest of the day with client meetings. It was later in the afternoon and Sophie had just received the call logs for the office and was about to go through them when she picked up an incoming call on Zach's line. Usually he diverted his calls to his cell phone when he was out, because the nature of his work meant he needed to be accessible to his clients, so Sophie was surprised to see his line light up.

"Zach Lassiter's office, this is Sophie speaking," she answered crisply.

"Mr. Lassiter, please," a male voice responded.

"I'm sorry, he's unable to take your call. I could get him to phone when he's available. Who's calling, please?"

"No, I won't leave a message, thanks."

And just like that, the call ended. Sophie couldn't quite put her finger on it, but something about the call, about the man making the call, set off her suspicions. She made a note on a message pad and tried to put it out of her mind for now, but curiosity kept pecking at her like a demented hen. There'd been noise in the caller's background, busy noise, and a voice over a PA system if she wasn't mistaken, paging someone. She closed her eyes and replayed the call in the back of her mind, but for the life of her she couldn't filter through the sounds to identify anything conclusive.

"Dreaming of me?"

Zach's voice startled her and her eyes flew open.

"Oh, always," she answered dryly. "You just missed a call, by the way. He wouldn't leave a message."

Zach flicked a glance at his watch. "Darn, I'd hoped to be here in time for that. Never mind, I'll give them a call back."

So he'd been expecting the call? Sophie tried to ignore the frisson of unease that raised the hairs on the back of her neck as he turned his back on her and went to his office and firmly closed the door behind him. Whatever it was he expected to discuss, it wasn't something he wanted her to overhear—again.

She forced her attention to the call logs, coding them as she went so the accounts department could apportion them accordingly. Alex had been a stickler for detail and while this was the kind of work normally assigned to someone on a far lower pay scale than Sophie's, he'd insisted it be part of her duties. So many of the numbers were familiar to her already, being those of people she knew who lived in and around Royal, but there was a new number cropping up in there over and over again. Sophie flicked back through the pages. There was no sign of that number being called while Alex had still been at the office, in fact, it appeared to be something that had only begun to occur recently and only from Zach's line.

Curious, Sophie picked up her phone and dialed the number.

"Good afternoon, you've reached the Philmore Clinic, how may I help you?"

"I'm sorry, I've dialed the wrong number."

Sophie put the phone down and turned to her computer, searching for the clinic. Her breath caught in her throat as the results lined up on her screen. She clicked on the main one, the website of the Philmore Clinic itself. Her eyes flicked across the screen as she read the home page, then more on the "about us" section of the site. It seemed the center was one for rehabilitation but also housed a secure-care facility for patients deemed mentally unstable and a danger to themselves or others.

Her thoughts boggled on the information even as she closed the window on her computer. Was that where Alex was? Had Zach somehow had him committed? Surely not. He wouldn't have been able to do something like that without medical intervention in some form, and surely if Alex had been unstable she or others would have noticed something, seen some warning signs. Maybe Zach just had a client who worked from there. Yes, that's what it had to be, she tried to convince herself. But even so, a little niggle of concern continued to hover at the back of her mind.

Maybe she should just ask Zach outright, she thought, her pen still hovering over the numbers. He came out of his office—his face drawn and his short hair rumpled, as if he'd been running his fingers through it—and his laptop case in his hand.

"Something's come up," he said heading for the main office door. "I'm going to a meeting, and I probably won't be back to the office tonight."

"Before you go, can you check this off for me? It's a number I can't code on the call log."

He strode over to her desk and swiveled the paper around to face him. "Just code it to me, personally," he said, his face grim.

"Personally," she repeated.

"Yeah, anything else?"

"Um, no," she replied, stung a little by his abruptness. Last night and this morning, Zach had been a different man altogether. It was clear something was bothering him. "Except, is there anything I can help you out with?"

"I wish you could, but no."

"Well, when do you expect to be back?" she asked, pressing gently for some kind of response that might give her an insight as to where he was going. "I thought maybe I could cook for you tonight, at my place."

"I'm sorry, I can't. I have no idea of when I'll be free tonight, so better not make plans. I'll pick you up tomorrow evening for the TCC event, okay? Look, I'm sorry I have to race out now. I'd hoped…"

"Don't worry. I understand."

Sophie interrupted before he delivered some platitude she couldn't bear to hear and while she mouthed

the words of understanding, she did so without sentiment. She didn't understand. Not one bit. Where had
the man she'd spent the night with gone? She'd thought
they were maybe at the start of something new together.
Something they both wanted. But here she was—left
staring at the door as he went out to the main office and
then, presumably, off to his unexpected meeting, leaving her with far more questions than answers.

Nine

Zach watched with mixed emotions as the other members of the TCC circulated around the room. Pride swirled foremost among them. That a boy from a middle-class upbringing could count membership in the Texas Cattleman's Club among his achievements was something else. His dad would be puffed up with pride when he heard.

He made a mental note to call his parents on Sunday at their retirement villa in Florida. A villa he'd bought for them, pushing past his father's stubborn pride, which wouldn't allow him to accept Zach's offer of relocating them to their dream destination. But Zach had been firm. He wanted them to be able to enjoy their retirement years—they'd both worked so hard all their lives to create a stable and happy home for him. Even when his dad had been made redundant from his work at an electronics design and manufacturing firm, they'd scraped by to make ends meet, refusing to touch the money they'd set aside for Zach's college education even though doing so would have lightened their load considerably. It was the least he could do to see them into comfortable and carefree years now.

Yeah, his dad would be proud of him, all right. But the man he'd most wanted to have by his side tonight wasn't here, and that troubled him deeply. Judging by the slightly more somber tone to the evening, he wasn't the only one who felt that way. Alex's disappearance remained the hot topic of conversation.

"Zach, now that the formalities are over, let me personally welcome you to the club." Gil Addison, the club president, extended his hand.

Zach shook it warmly. "Thank you. I'm honored to be a member."

"I see you're here with Sophie Beldon. She's Alex Santiago's assistant, isn't she?"

"And mine until he gets back," Zach said, his eyes finding Sophie across the room.

She was dressed in a simple black dress in a wraparound style that had him eager to unwrap her the minute he had her to himself. Before picking her up this evening, he'd called and left a message to suggest she bring an overnight bag and stay at his place. He hadn't realized just how much he'd been hoping she'd agree until he'd arrived at her apartment and seen the bag just inside the front door.

"You still think he's coming back?"

"I sure hope so."

"I take it you haven't heard any more?"

Zach shook his head. "Nothing."

Gil nodded. "It's a puzzle all right. I understand Nate Battle has been coordinating with a state investigator out of Dallas. I imagine she'll be in touch with you at some stage, too. Since you two worked together."

"Glad to hear the sheriff is making the most of all resources."

"Yeah. The investigator, Bailey Collins, seems to believe that Alex Santiago may not even be his real name. Kinda makes you wonder who he really is."

"And where," Zach added, shocked to hear that his friend might not be who he said he was.

Given the nature of their business and the massive volumes of money they handled on behalf of their clients, the news set alarm bells ringing in Zach's head. He knew the police had frozen Alex's personal accounts and the business accounts were running as normal at the moment, but he made a mental note to change the passwords again just to be certain. While they changed their passwords regularly, they were done in a system that Alex was familiar with. If he turned out to be some kind of criminal, they ran the risk of losing everything, especially with the Manson project about to go live in another week with a massive cash injection from investors.

"Let me know if you hear anything else," Gil asked before excusing himself as someone gestured to him from the other side of the room.

Sophie cut through the crowd to his side and Zach pushed aside his concerns about Alex to mull over later on.

"Enjoying yourself? It's quite a turnout for the new member welcome ceremony, isn't it?"

The night almost read like a who's who of Royal. Longtime TCC member Beau Hacket sat at a table with a bunch of his cronies—many of whom, he'd heard, had objected vociferously to Abigail Price's run for the club presidency a couple of years ago. Beau's wife, Barbara, mingled with a group of older women who'd circled around her daughter, Lila, and another TCC member, Sam Gordon. And those were just a few of the faces he knew or recognized.

"Sure is," Zach agreed. "Do you want to stay for the dancing?"

"Is that what you want to do?" she asked, looking up at him with those sinfully sexy whiskey-colored eyes.

Her eye makeup was a burnished gold, emphasizing the width and beauty of her gaze and Zach met the unspoken question in her eyes with an answering twist deep in his groin.

"Not by any stretch of the imagination, unless—" he bent to speak privately in the shell of her ear "—you and I are dancing naked."

He felt her shiver in response. "Then, in the interests of not scandalizing the company we're in, I'd say we should make our apologies and go, wouldn't you?"

Zach couldn't have agreed more. He reached for her hand and they began to make their way out of the room, stopping here and there to shake a hand or exchange a brief farewell. He'd brought the Cadillac coupe tonight and after the valet pulled the car to the entrance of the club for him, he ushered Sophie into her seat, getting an eyeful of her décolletage at the same time. She wasn't wearing a bra.

His mouth went dry, his fingers spasmed into a tight grip on the edge of the car door. In an instant he'd gone from semiaroused to rock hard, his pulse throbbing with all the pent-up longing of a flamenco guitar. He couldn't wait to find out what other surprises she had for him under that dress. He forced himself to let go of the door and close it before walking around the car and easing himself into the driver's seat.

Sophie, oblivious to his discomfort, flung him a smile in the darkened interior as he crawled past the cars lining the driveway and out onto the road. He completed the journey back to his place in record time—prepared to risk a speeding violation to get her home before the top of his head exploded, not to mention other parts of his body.

Not bothering to garage the coupe, he climbed from the car and grabbed Sophie's overnight bag from the trunk. She was waiting on the front step as he slammed it closed. He pressed his finger on the biometric scanner to allow him access to the house and to disable the alarm and forced himself to draw in a deep breath. They had all night and all day tomorrow. He could take his time, he could savor every second with Sophie rather than rush at her like the randy teenager who suddenly seemed to have control of his mind. And his body.

"It's a beautiful night, isn't it?" Sophie said, inhaling the night air redolent with the scent of the standard roses that lined the turning bay of the driveway.

He stopped a second and looked at her. Really looked. She all but glowed, the exterior lighting making her blond hair a shining cap of palest spun gold.

"You know what's beautiful," he responded, coming up the steps to stand beside her, "you."

He bent his head and kissed her, long and deep and wet, until he felt her tremble beneath him. It took all of his control not to drop her bag and sweep her off her feet and carry her to the nearest soft horizontal surface, but somehow he managed it.

"Come on inside. Would you like a drink before we go to bed?"

Surprise flitted across her face ever so briefly and he contained an inner smile. It was good to know she was as eager as he was to make it up to the master suite, but a little more anticipation never hurt anybody, even though certain parts of his body were making their objections to that statement well known right now.

"Sure, that'd be nice."

"Let's go outside," he suggested. "There's a wet bar in the loggia by the pool."

He placed her bag near the bottom of the staircase and took her by the hand again, leading her through the house and out to the pool terrace.

"Oh, my goodness!" Sophie exclaimed. "I never realized you had all this here behind the house."

He smiled. "The last time you were here we didn't exactly make time for the full tour, did we?"

A flush spread over her cheeks in response. "No, we didn't. Seriously, though, Zach. All this for one person?"

"It's an investment," he said as they crossed the terrace to the loggia and he gestured for her to sit down in one of the deep, cushioned wicker chairs facing the massive stone fireplace he'd commissioned for when the weather began to cool.

"Some investment," she muttered. "What's that way?"

Zach followed where her finger pointed down a colonnaded walkway. "My fitness center and spa, and beyond that there's a private putting green for when I'm entertaining clients. What would you like to drink? Champagne or something stronger?"

"Oh, champagne, please. You've entertained clients here?"

"I've had a few visitors stay in the guest house."

He popped the cork of the bottle he'd withdrawn from the wine fridge under the bar and poured two glasses. Sophie had risen from her seat and drifted over closer to the pool and even now was bending down to trail her fingers in the clear water.

"It feels like silk," she said, straightening and accepting the glass from him as he drew closer.

"Did you feel like a swim?"

"I didn't bring a suit."

"There are plenty in the changing rooms, but, with no neighbors for at least a couple of acres and no staff on duty except you and me," he said, clinking his glass to hers and taking a sip of the foaming golden liquid, "suits are entirely optional."

Sophie looked at him for a moment and allowed the sip of champagne she'd taken to trickle past the restriction of her throat. The idea of swimming naked with Zach all but made her throat close up in anticipation. The night air was still warm, the water of the pool just right. Beneath her dress she felt her nipples harden, her insides clench on a rolling pull that started deep inside her body and radiated out to her extremities.

She'd never done anything so risqué or erotic before in her life, never wanted to. But she couldn't think of anything she'd rather do right here, right now with the gorgeous man standing in this unbelievable setting with her.

"Well," she said, stepping out of his hold and placing her champagne flute carefully on a nearby patio table, "since suits are optional…"

She saw his fingers clench on the slender stem of his glass as her hands went to the knot at the side of her dress. Very slowly, she worked the fabric loose and unwrapped the gown from her body. She'd prevaricated over what to wear beneath it all day, but the lady in the shop had suggested she go braless—something she couldn't remember doing in polite company since she was about twelve years old.

At home she'd realized she really didn't have any other choice. The undergarment would have spoiled the visual line of the front of the dress and the way it was bound around her it provided sufficient support for her breasts. Her skin tingled on exposure to the night air that gently moved around them, laden with herbaceous scents from the manicured gardens that surrounded them.

Sophie's eyes flew to Zach's face. He was staring straight at her, his jaw clenched, his eyes shimmering. She let go of the ties and wriggled her shoulders, feeling the silk of her dress slide down her back to fall behind her, leaving her exposed in only her black lace panties, sheer black thigh-high stockings and her patent high-heeled pumps.

One by one, she stepped out of her shoes then, resting first one foot and then the other on a nearby lounger, she slowly rolled down her stockings. She flicked a glance at Zach. He hadn't moved so much as an inch and she could see the cords of his neck standing out prominently as he clearly battled to keep himself under control. A bulge behind the fabric of his trousers left her no doubt just how strained that control was right now.

With a private smile she hooked her thumbs in the waistband of her panties and slowly slid them off her hips. A strangled sound escaped his throat as she turned away from him and leaned over the table to pick up her wine, taking another sip before replacing the glass

OFFICIAL OPINION POLL

Dear Reader,

Since you are a book enthusiast, we would like to know what you think.

Inside you will find a short Opinion Poll. Please participate in our Poll by sharing your opinion on 3 subjects that are very important to all of us.

To thank you for your participation, we would like to send you **2 FREE BOOKS** and **2 FREE GIFTS!**

Please enjoy them with our compliments.

Sincerely,

Pam Powers

YOUR OPINION POLL
THANK-YOU FREE GIFTS INCLUDE:

▶ **2 HARLEQUIN DESIRE® BOOKS**

▶ **2 LOVELY SURPRISE GIFTS**

OFFICIAL OPINION POLL

YOUR OPINION COUNTS!
Please check TRUE or FALSE below to express your opinion about the following statements:

Q1 Do you believe in "true love"?

"TRUE LOVE HAPPENS ONLY ONCE IN A LIFETIME."
○ TRUE
○ FALSE

Q2 Do you think marriage has any value in today's world?

"YOU CAN BE TOTALLY COMMITTED TO SOMEONE WITHOUT BEING MARRIED."
○ TRUE
○ FALSE

Q3 What kind of books do you enjoy?

"A GREAT NOVEL MUST HAVE A HAPPY ENDING."
○ TRUE
○ FALSE

YES! I have placed my sticker in the space provided below. Please send me the **2 FREE** books and **2 FREE** gifts for which I qualify. I understand that I am under no obligation to purchase anything further, as explained on the back of this card.

225/326 HDL F4WP

FIRST NAME

LAST NAME

ADDRESS

APT.#

CITY

STATE/PROV.

ZIP/POSTAL CODE

HD-TF-09/13

Printed in the U.S.A. © 2013 HARLEQUIN ENTERPRISES LIMITED.

® and ™ are trademarks owned and used by the trademark owner and/or its licensee.

once more. As she stood, Sophie ran her tongue around her lips.

"Mmm, I really like that," she said and sauntered toward the edge of the pool before flinging another glance his way once she was poised at the edge. "So, are you joining me?"

Without waiting for a response, she executed a perfect dive into the silky water, relishing the sensation of it over her naked body. She'd barely made it to the end of the pool before a splash alerted her she had company. A rumpled pile of clothing lay where Zach had previously stood, and a dark shadow now approached her beneath the water.

Sophie put her feet down, relieved to discover she could touch the base of the pool, and waited for him to break the surface. She didn't have to wait long. Zach's arms caught around her middle and dragged her to him, his mouth closing on hers in a hungry caress that left her in no doubt that her little striptease had driven him to the edge.

She lifted her feet and clasped her legs around his hips, his erection trapped between their bodies.

"Do you feel what you do to me?" he growled against her mouth.

He lifted her slightly so her breasts were free of the water and buried his face against them. She shuddered at the feel of his lips, his tongue delving into the valley created when she'd clasped her arms around his shoulders. She tilted her head back a little, thrusting her chest out, her breasts aching for more.

Zach's hands loosened their grasp at her waist and slid up the ridges of her rib cage, slowly rising up her body to cup her tender globes. The ache inside her intensified as his mouth, so hot compared to the lukewarm water of the pool, closed around one tightly beaded nipple. His tongue swirled the sensitive tip, his lips suckling, his teeth gently rasping until she squirmed against him.

She felt the heavy ridge of his desire against her entrance and tilted her hips to stroke his length with her body. She craved him with a force she had never felt before, her entire being attuned to him, his breath on her skin, his heat against her body, his hardness against that part of her that was soft and willing and compliant—begging for his possession.

He completed his worship of her breasts, his hands dropping down now to cup her buttocks, to lift her ever so slightly higher so his erection sprang free, no longer trapped between them. Sophie clung to Zach's shoulders as he positioned her over him, as he slowly began to lower her down. She felt the blunt tip of him probing her body and she gasped her pleasure as he slowly filled her. He waited, allowing her body to adjust around him or simply to rein in some control; she could feel his muscles straining as if he was holding back.

"Let go, Zach," she whispered against his ear, and she flicked her tongue out to caress his earlobe before catching the neat nub of flesh between her teeth and biting gently. "Let go."

His fingers tightened on her buttocks and she felt the muscles in his thighs bunch beneath her before he withdrew slightly then surged back again. Sophie loosened her grip on his shoulders and caught his face in her hands, sealing his lips with hers and putting all her desire, all her hopes, all her dreams into her kiss. Her tongue caught and dueled with his and she suckled against it, drawing it gently into her mouth before letting him go and doing it all again. Zach moved again, this time settling deeper than before. She felt as if he knocked at the door to her soul as the first ripples of pleasure began to radiate out from her core, as her thighs clenched tight about him as she broke off their kiss to drop her head back.

A sharp cry ripped from her throat as those ripples sharpened, deepened into something even more concentrated, more powerful than anything she'd experienced before—as her body began to shake and all but implode on the bliss that ripped her from reality and flung her into a sea of sensual gratification far richer than her dreams.

Zach's mouth fastened on her where her neck flared to meet her shoulder, his teeth sinking ever so gently into her skin. All her nerves concentrated on that one spot, heightening her consciousness as he ground his lower body against her, as he drove her toward yet another peak. This time her climax was more gentle, more indulgent—and as she welcomed the rolling sense of completion that spread through her body once more, she felt Zach stiffen and tremble in her arms, his head now resting in the crook of her neck, his breath coming in sharp gasps against her skin.

It was several minutes before she could move, before she even wanted to move, but eventually Sophie untangled her legs from their grip around his hips. Zach lifted her off his body before gathering her tightly to him.

"I can't get enough of you," he admitted softly in the night air.

"I feel the same way," she answered, spreading her hands across his chest, feeling his heart hammering in his chest at a rate similar to her own.

Sophie's feet found the floor of the pool and she was grateful for the buoyancy of the water and Zach's steadying embrace, because she doubted she'd have been capable of standing on her own otherwise.

"Good, let's go and rinse off and head inside."

Zach guided her to the steps at the corner of the pool and together they ascended onto the patio. Sophie was surprised when she saw the outdoor shower, with multiple heads, set off to one side of the loggia and changing rooms. Although she wondered why she was surprised, since Zach had surrounded himself with the very best of everything.

Suddenly, despite her boldness these past few days, a small kernel of doubt invaded her mind. She knew she'd virtually thrown herself at him the other night in the office, but he'd chosen to take her out with him tonight. If a man like Zach only indulged in the best, what was he doing with her?

Ten

Zach felt Sophie's withdrawal as if it was a physical thing. Up until now they'd been so in tune with one another, yet he could feel her pulling away—mentally, if not physically.

Determined to get to the bottom of it, he turned off the shower faucets and walked a short distance to the changing room to grab towels and robes. Sophie followed him and grabbed a towel off the stack and began to dry herself.

"Here," he said, taking the towel from her, "let me."

"It's okay, I can—"

"I want to, Sophie."

She submitted to his request and once he'd finished drying her and helped her into a fluffy white robe, he swiftly dried himself off. Then, collecting their champagne and glasses, he showed her back inside.

"You hungry?" he asked.

"A little bit," she admitted with one of those sweet smiles of hers. "That was quite a workout."

He loved the way color stung her cheeks when she was embarrassed.

He led the way into the kitchen and pulled out a bar stool for her. As she sat down, he topped off their wineglasses and lifted his in a toast.

"To us," he said, "and a great weekend."

She lifted her glass also but remained silent.

"What is it, Sophie? What's the matter?" he asked.

He hadn't been imagining it out by the pool. Something was definitely playing on her mind. Something he'd rather she shove out in the open now so they could deal with it and move on.

"Nothing's the matter," she denied, taking a sip of her wine and firing a smile at him that could have fooled a man who hadn't made an art form over the past couple weeks out of watching her and finding out what made her tick.

He'd felt a pull of something toward Sophie when he'd started working with Alex but, as raw as he was after his son's death and the finality of his divorce he hadn't been ready to take a step in that direction. Now, though, was an entirely different matter. With the distance of time acting as a buffer, Sophie Beldon had brought so many aspects of him back to aching life.

"There's something. You've been fine up until just a while ago. Is it something someone said tonight? Something I said, or did?"

"No! It's not you. Seriously, it's not you. You're... well, you're perfect," she ended softly, her eyes downcast.

He snorted inelegantly. "I'm hardly perfect."

"But you are. You're successful, you have this amazing home. You can have just about anything money can buy and probably just about anything it can't."

He was puzzled. "And that's a problem?"

"Why me, Zach? Out of all the women you could have taken out with you tonight, of all the women you could sleep with, why me?"

He stilled, forcing himself to take his time answering her. He moved across the kitchen, grabbing a half loaf of French bread and slicing it into medallions and then taking some sliced cold cuts, relish and fresh cheese from the refrigerator. He laid the food on a platter and put it on the granite island where she was sitting before taking the seat beside her.

"Why you?" he repeated, lifting a hand to smooth an errant strand of hair from her beautiful, worried face. "Because deep down I know you're as lovely on the inside as you are on the outside. You forget, I've had over a year to get to know you, over a year feeling my way through my growing attraction to you. I'll be honest. As short a time as only a few weeks ago, I thought it would mess things up in the office if I acted on my feelings—not to mention complicate things in my already complicated world. But when you made it clear to me the other night that you felt the same way, that you wanted me, I knew I couldn't keep you at arm's length any longer."

He spread some ripe Brie onto a slice of bread and added a small dollop of relish before handing it to her. She remained silent, as if digesting what he'd said.

Zach continued. "And you talk about this place, my *amazing home*. It's not a home. It's where I live, sure, but it's not a home. I know what it takes to make a home and that is usually a family. I was lucky, I had that growing up. I had the security of having two parents who loved me and who I knew would move heaven and earth to give me every opportunity in the world to excel. And I have. I have excelled because I'm determined to always be the best I can be. Sure, I've taken risks. Some have paid off. Some haven't. I've learned to judge better what's right and what's wrong, and Sophie?" He reached out to cup her cheek, tracing the outline of her sensually full and wide lower lip with the edge of his thumb. "I mixed business with pleasure once before and it put me off ever wanting to do that again, but you, you're a risk I'm definitely ready to take. I want to know you better."

He leaned forward and kissed her, keeping it gentle, trying to imbue into his action what he suspected his words hadn't quite gotten through to her yet. When he broke off their kiss, her eyes glistened in the overhead lighting.

"Thank you," she said. "For being so honest."

"No problem," he answered with a quirk of his lip. "More to eat?"

"Yes, please. I'm suddenly starving."

The quirk spread into a smile. If she had an appetite, it was a good thing he knew exactly how to appease it. After they'd eaten and finished the champagne, they went upstairs to his room.

Zach turned down the bed while Sophie freshened up in the en suite bathroom. He reached for her as she walked back into the bedroom, tugging at the sash of her robe.

"In a hurry, Mr. Lassiter?" she asked teasingly, stepping just out of his reach.

"For you? Always."

And it was shockingly true. Since that first time they'd made love in his office, he'd been in a state of heightened awareness. A state of readiness that de-

manded to be assuaged. Not even last night's hurried
trip to meet with Dr. Philmore to discuss a potential
treatment plan for Anna had taken the edge off his craving for Sophie.

She stepped into the circle of his arms, her hands
going to the lapels of his robe and pushing them aside
and stroking across his chest. Her hands were silky soft
as they traced the definition of his pecs before track-
ing a line down the center of his chest and lower, to his
waist. Her fingers made quick work of the knot on his
robe and she let the garment hang loose as her hands
continued their voyage of discovery down his body.

He hissed in a breath when she reached his erection
and closed a fist around him.

"Ready for more, I see," she observed.

"Always willing to please," Zach replied, trying to
keep his voice light but failing miserably as his awareness of her touch, of the gentle pressure of her fingers,
increased by increments.

"This time I want to please you."

"You always please me, Sophie."

"I don't think you fully understand me," she sighed
with a wicked twinkle in her eyes, "but you will."

Before he could do anything to stop her, she'd sunk
to her knees. Strands of her fine blond hair caught on
the smattering of hair of his upper thighs, making him
all too aware of what she'd planned. His muscles taut-
ened, bracing themselves for what was to come. It didn't
stop the groan of sheer delight from escaping his throat
when her warm lips closed around the swollen head of
his penis. Or when her tongue stroked the underside of
the tip, where his skin was most sensitive. Sophie began
to move her head, to take him deeper into the warm,

wet cavern of her mouth, her lips and tongue continuing to cause flame after flame of heat to lick through him.

She made a sound deep in the back of her throat, a sound that sent a vibration rippling through him. It was his undoing. He'd planned to hold on, to maintain control, to take, but only so much—but with that one action she dominated him fully and his climax hit hard, unexpectedly, rocking him to the very center of his being.

As pulse after pulse pounded through him, she slowed her actions, the slick softness of her tongue now almost unbearable against his hypersensitized flesh. Almost, but not quite, he admitted as another jolt of completion made his hips jerk involuntarily. She let him go, stroking him once with her hand before rising to her feet.

Zach's heart was still pounding in his chest but he reached for her, closing her in the circle of his arms and holding her, his chin resting on the top of her golden head. She felt so perfect in his arms. How could he have continued to deny himself this?

Eventually he loosened his hold and sat on the bed, pulling Sophie down with him. They lay down together, facing one another.

"What did I do to deserve you?" he asked.

She smiled in return. "I've been asking myself that question all night."

Zach traced the edge of the lapel of her robe, delighting in the fine trail of goose bumps that followed the path of his fingertip. He moved in closer, flicking out his tongue to follow that same path down the V of her robe and then back up the other side.

"I think this should go, don't you?" he murmured, undoing her sash and tugging it loose.

Slowly he traced the outside edge of her robe with his tongue once more, then blew cool air from his mouth over her moistened skin. She gave a small shiver, one that had little to do with temperature, judging by the blush that now spread across her chest. Her breasts lifted on each breath she took and he followed their shape with his tongue, again blowing that cool air over her skin. Sophie's nipples grew tight and extended, their pink tips thrusting out. He kept up his gentle assault, touching her lightly each time, then blowing once again until she squirmed against the sheets.

"More, Zach. I need more," she implored him.

"In a hurry? You'll have to be patient. Now, where was I?"

It tormented him no less that he went back to the very beginning, commencing anew his tantalizing touches—each one awakening his body even as he knew it stoked hers to scorching life. Eventually, though, he could resist no longer. He had to feel her beneath his hands and he eased the robe off her shoulders, spreading the fabric wide on either side of her, exposing her nakedness for his eyes to feast on.

She moaned and pressed into his hands as he cupped her breasts, kneading them gently, his mouth alternating from one distended tip to the other. Beneath him he felt her legs move restlessly and he settled between them, one knee drawing up to her core. She was hot and wet against him, and it took every ounce of his considerable control not to simply take her there and then.

Zach began a journey down her body, forcing himself to take his time, to make sure that every caress, every touch brought her new waves of enjoyment. By the time he reached the delicate hollow at the top of her thighs, that enticing arrowed apex, he could smell her sweet, musky scent. It made everything in his body clench tight.

"You're torturing me, Zach," she said breathlessly. Her hands reaching for him, her fingers knotting in his hair.

"That's the plan," he said with a smile and lowered his lips to her heat.

She all but lifted off the bed as he closed his mouth around her, as his tongue unerringly found the pearl of nerve endings that he knew would drive her crazy, mad, over the edge. He wasn't wrong. His touch was like a match set to paper; she was a skyrocket waiting to be set free. Her body bowed, her hips lifting off the bed, her legs clamped tight around his shoulders as he swirled his tongue around that tiny bud of flesh, as his lips tugged and pulled, until with a scream of abandon she hurtled over the edge and into orgasm.

She was still a supple mass of limbs and torso when he pushed himself up over her, when he guided his length within her swollen, still-contracting center. Zach laced his fingers through hers, lifted her hands up, holding them beside her head. It was as if a line drew all the way down his spine to where they connected. Down his spine and then back up hers again, as if they were always meant to be this perfect together. Sophie's eyes flew wide open.

"Oh, my Lord. Again?"

Her climax chased the surprise from her eyes and she shuddered against him, her fingers now so tight around his own he'd begun to lose feeling in them. Her powerful, rhythmic contractions were enough to tip him completely over the edge, his climax drawing from the soles of his feet and reverberating through his body until he collapsed on top of her, breathless, stunned, pleasured beyond his imagination.

Sophie woke several hours later. It was still dark outside. She reached for Zach but she was alone, his side of the bed warm but very definitely empty. There was no light from the bathroom, either. She started a little as the bedroom door opened. Zach slid, naked, into the bed.

"Are you okay?" she whispered.

"Better than I've ever been," he said, feeling for her hand and lifting it to his lips to kiss it.

"Me, too," she sighed in satisfaction. "But how come you're awake? Can't sleep?"

Zach settled onto his back and she snuggled up against his chest.

"No, I can't stop thinking about Alex. Wondering where the hell he is and what might have happened to him."

"I know. It's never far from anyone's thoughts these days. So many people were discussing it at the club tonight. I hope he's going to be okay."

"Gil told me that the sheriff has brought in a state investigator from Dallas. She believes that Alex Santiago isn't even his real name."

Sophie stiffened. "Seriously?" Her mind raced. "You don't think he could be a fraud, do you? I'd find it hard to believe. It just doesn't jell with the guy we know and have worked with."

"I know. He's my friend and I'm worried now that maybe I didn't know him after all. But what worries me most is that, for one reason or another, someone's hurt him, badly. Otherwise I know he'd have done everything in his power to come back to us here in Royal. He has too much here to simply walk away from it.

"For a while there this evening I got angry, and started to consider it might be true, that he is a fraud. But I've been playing it over in my mind and it just doesn't fit."

Sophie lay quietly, listening to the confusion and frustration in Zach's voice and wishing she could do more to alleviate his concern. He certainly didn't sound like the kind of guy who could be involved in his friend's disappearance. If he was, he was a very good actor. She eschewed that idea the instant it came to her mind—the one that made her so anal about dotting every *i* and crossing every *t*—just wouldn't let it go.

That devil demanded one hundred percent certainty and it made Sophie nothing if not persistent, a trait her mother had frequently complained of while Sophie had been growing up. But it had gotten her where she was in life today; it had helped her growing up more times than she could remember, especially after Susannah had gone. And now as an adult, it had stood her in good stead as she fought to find her sister.

"What if you're wrong, Zach? What if he is a fraud, a very good one? People fool other people all the time."

As he could be fooling her right now.

"Yeah, I can't discount that. To be on the safe side I've just been online to change the password sequence for the bank accounts. With the Manson project going live soon, there is going to be a lot of money transferring through those accounts starting Monday. I can't risk anything happening to our investors' funds."

"Oh, Lord. I didn't even think about that."

Zach held her close. "Don't worry, I'm sure it would never come to anything."

They lay together, quiet in the darkness. After a while, Sophie realized that Zach had drifted off to sleep. She wasn't as lucky, as their short conversation kept playing around in her head, keeping her awake. So Alex might not have been who he said he was, but who was Zach Lassiter, exactly? He hadn't grown up here in Royal. No one really knew his background, a background that he kept very close to his chest.

It was still within the realm of possibility that he might have had something to do with Alex's disappearance, for all that he'd sounded genuinely concerned only moments ago. Maybe he'd even locked up Alex at that clinic he'd been in contact with so often. And now he'd changed the banking passwords. Sure, it made sense if he was genuinely concerned about Alex accessing funds illegally, but who was to say that it wasn't Zach who planned to do the exact same thing?

Sophie's stomach churned and she eased herself away from his sleeping form. All joking aside, had she just begun to sleep with the enemy?

Eleven

Logic warred with instinct. Instinct told her, over and over, that Zach couldn't be involved—that he was genuinely concerned for his friend. Logic told to her to make sure.

But how? All she'd managed to find out so far was he had been calling a private clinic frequently and very recently. He could have an investment client there for all she knew. She discarded the thought as soon as it popped into her head. Zach had a standard procedure for new clients, one that had always involved her creating a personal file for the client in their computer system. If his calls had been work related, she would have known. Besides, hadn't he told her only yesterday to mark those calls to his personal expense when she queried them on the call log?

He was up to something. Everything inside her said so. But what was it? His laptop! He carried it with him everywhere. If she could access his computer, she was sure she could find out just what was going on.

Sophie slipped from the bed and grabbed one of the robes off the bedroom floor. She stilled in her actions as Zach muttered something in his sleep and rolled over. In seconds he was breathing deeply again. She walked carefully across the thickly carpeted floor and let herself out of the room.

Where would be the most logical place to look for his computer, she wondered. She hadn't seen it in the kitchen when they'd been in there, but just off the kitchen was a high-tech den that had looked well used. Since every other area of the house appeared to be in show-home condition, she kept her fingers crossed that when Zach was home he used his den as more of a family room or office.

A trickle of unease ran through her as she made her way down the curved staircase to the ground floor and walked across the tiles toward the back of the house. She was going out on a very shaky limb doing this. Chances were she'd find nothing incriminating at all. At least she fervently hoped not.

Thankful that the outdoor lighting cast enough light through the floor-to-ceiling downstairs windows that she didn't need to turn on any lights, Sophie made her way through to the den. Long plush sofas faced one another across a large marble coffee table and two deep armchairs were positioned at one end, facing the large-screen television mounted on the wall above the fireplace. It was a cozy room, even in the semidark but, she reminded herself, she wasn't there to admire the decor.

Her eyes, now well adjusted to the half light, scanned the room. Yes! Right there, on the table, sat his computer. He'd left it open, obviously in a hurry to get back to bed after he'd secured the new passwords on the bank accounts. Had he simply let it go into sleep mode, or had he shut it down completely, she wondered, picking her way through the furniture. She really wanted to get this over with as quickly as possible. She had no idea how long it would be before he realized she was missing from the bed.

Sophie lowered herself onto the sofa and placed her finger on the mouse pad, a sigh of relief sawing through her as the screen brightened and came to life. She keyed in Zach's password, one he'd given her several months ago when he'd needed her to retrieve data for him on a rare occasion that he'd left the computer behind in the office.

She caught her lower lip between her teeth, worrying at the tender flesh as she decided where the best place to start looking for information might be. Email or general files? Email, she decided, and opened the program, then quickly typed *Philmore Center* into the search window.

As she did so, a worrying thought occurred to her. She'd been so quick to suspect Zach of some wrongdoing, but what if he was in contact with the Philmore Center because of something wrong with *his* health? A sharp stab of concern struck her square in her chest. He was always such a loner, mixing but never really socializing, always working long hours.

Alex had probably been his closest friend, and Alex was missing. Had Alex discovered something about Zach and his past, his mental health even, that Zach wasn't happy about? Sophie tried to quell her overactive mind and focus instead on the results that had come up from her search. There were several emails both to and from the Philmore Center. She scrolled down to the earliest one, dated only days after Alex was last seen.

She opened the email and began to read. The more she read, the angrier she became. Okay, so her investigating hadn't led her to any answers about Alex Santiago's whereabouts, but it had certainly led her into some new insights into Zach's character. From the looks of things, despite no support from the rest of her family, he was about to commit his ex-wife into a mental institution. She'd heard of some crazy things in her time but what kind of man did that to his ex?

He didn't know what had woken him, but Zach was surprised to discover he was alone in his bed. He waited a few minutes, but Sophie didn't return from wherever she'd gone. Dawn was still some time away, so he doubted she'd woken hungry and gone looking for food. He rose from the bed and grabbed a pair of sweatpants from his drawer, hoisting them to his hips before heading out of the room. No lights on anywhere, he noticed, his concern rising. Had she gotten up and headed downstairs, only to fall somewhere?

He checked each of the formal rooms off the main entrance. No, no sign of her there. The kitchen, maybe? As he entered the kitchen, he heard a click from the den. What the…?

He stopped in the doorway, watching Sophie as, with her face lit from the computer screen, she clicked and scrolled her way through something. A cold, burning fury lit deep inside of him. He should have known she was too good to be true. What was her angle, he wondered. And what the hell was she finding so damn interesting on his laptop? He stepped forward. Sophie was so engrossed in what was on the screen she didn't hear or see him. He stepped closer, looking at the computer screen as he did so. She was reading his private email.

Zach moved swiftly, leaning over her, his hand reaching for the laptop and closing it with a snap. Sophie jumped backward against the sofa before rising swiftly to her feet.

"What do you think you're doing?" Zach asked, working double time to keep his voice low and even.

It was no small feat, given the wild anger and sense of betrayal that warred for supremacy inside him. To his absolute surprise, though, instead of making some excuse or even some apology, Sophie blasted straight back at him with both barrels.

"More to the point, what on earth do you think *you're* doing? I knew there was something up with you, I just knew it. I thought it had something to do with Alex, but it's worse than that."

"Worse?" Zach gripped the back of the sofa with both hands to stop himself from reaching for her and giving her a darn good shake. "What could be worse than a friend, a well-respected businessman, going missing for no apparent reason?"

"Locking your wife into an institution and throwing away the key, for one!"

Zach straightened and shoved a hand through his hair. "This is ridiculous. You don't even know what you're talking about."

"I've read enough to see that you want her out of your hair. You forget, I've fielded her phone calls to you. I've seen how distant you are afterward. For whatever reason, she's still very dependent on you. You even mention it in your emails to Dr. Philmore. I used to think it was strange that you two still had so much contact together since your divorce, and clearly you do, too. I guess you've had enough, haven't you? Why else would you be planning to lock her away? Don't you think that's just a bit too draconian?"

"Draconian?" He shook his head slowly, his cynicism clear in the smile he gave her. "You really have no idea."

"You think?" Sophie replied with a snap, her arms crossed tight in front of her. "Well, let me tell you, it looks like you want her out of your hair. You want her institutionalized. How on earth can you even consider such an act against her?"

"Maybe to save her life?" Zach shot back. "I told you, you have no idea what you're talking about. Anna is a danger to herself. She's already made a couple of unsuccessful attempts on her life since our son died two years ago."

"Your son?" Sophie looked shocked. "You have a son?"

"Had," he corrected. "He died six weeks after he and his mother were in a car wreck. He was only ten months old. Anna lost control of her car on a wet road and slid sideways into a bridge abutment."

The words he spoke were simple, yet every one tore at his heart again as if the loss had been only yesterday.

"A-and Anna?" Sophie asked, sinking onto the chair again.

"She walked away with nothing but whiplash and more guilt than any parent should ever have to bear."

"Oh, my Lord. That's awful."

"She'd been trying to teach me a lesson that night. Showing me that she wouldn't be there waiting for me when I came home late. That she wasn't at my beck and call. Things had been strained between us before Blake was conceived, in fact we'd already begun sepa-ration proceedings when she discovered she was pregnant." Zach dropped onto one of the sofas and leaned his elbows on his thighs, his head dropping between his shoulders, the weight of all that had gone wrong in his marriage like a millstone around his neck. "We'd argued on the phone when she told me she was going out. I'd warned her the roads were tricky, to just wait until I got home—that we'd talk then. But she wouldn't listen."

The memory burned, painful and fresh in his mind. His mad dash home to discover her car gone from the garage, the house empty—worse, Blake's crib empty when he should have been tucked up asleep with his favorite teddy.

"I didn't know where to begin to look for her, but I didn't have to wait long. The police came to my door within minutes of me getting home. She was hysterical, they said, but that was nothing compared to the quiet after she was released from the hospital. Her parents just put it down to grief, both for Blake and for our marriage when she insisted we continue with the divorce we'd begun almost two years prior, but it was much more than that. She'd always been fragile, but losing Blake, being responsible for his death, that broke something inside her."

Zach dragged in a deep breath and let it out again before continuing. "It's nearly two years exactly since Blake died and Anna went missing this week. I was fearing the worst. Thankfully she's turned up again, but I'm not prepared to take that risk again that next time she won't turn up and that it'll be a policeman instead, on her parents' doorstep or mine, telling us that this time she's succeeded in taking her own life. She desperately needs help before it's too late. I'm determined she will receive it."

"Zach, I'm sorry. I really don't know what to say."

Sophie's voice sounded small. She looked small, as if she'd retreated in on herself. All her anger against him had dissipated in the face of what he'd told her.

But his anger had not. It welled anew and filled his heart, where he'd begun to care, begun to think that perhaps with Sophie he could think about a new start, a new relationship.

"There's nothing you can say, now, is there? You know, if you had any questions, all you had to do was ask me. You didn't need to go snooping behind my back."

"I thought you were hiding something to do with Alex. I never had any idea that you were trying to help your wife."

"My *ex*-wife," he corrected, but then her words slowly sank in. "You actually thought I had something to do with Alex's disappearance? You slept with me, thinking that I might be responsible—perhaps even for Alex's death? Oh, yeah, that's right. You were prepared to come at me, guns blazing, over putting Anna in a secure unit. Of course you'd suspect me of doing something terrible to Alex." He stood up and shook his head in disbelief seasoned with a fair dose of disgust. "What kind of woman are you? I thought we had the start of something special but you were just using me, weren't you?"

"Zach, I'm sorry, I didn't know," she protested, also rising to her feet, throwing her hands out as if imploring him to believe her.

"But you believed I might be capable of it. What were you planning to do? *Seduce* the information out of me?"

He watched as her face flamed with color—as her eyes dropped, unable to meet his accusing gaze a second longer.

"You were so secretive. I know I should have known better, should have trusted you, but every time I'd come into your office you'd obscure your computer screen or cover the mouthpiece on your phone if you were on a call. I don't know." She shook her head. "In light of everything that had happened, I just started to get suspicious. And while it started that way, with wanting to seduce information out of you, it's not like that now."

"You seriously expect me to believe that when I've just walked in on you on my laptop reading my private email? Excuse me if I find your protestations just a little hard to believe. Besides, don't you think the police questioned me thoroughly enough? You thought you possibly knew more than them or at least enough to believe I was guilty of doing something so stupid?"

"I'm so sorry, Zach. Please forgive me. Like I said, I should have known better. What you're trying to do for Anna is noble and kind and good. Just like you are. I can see that. I could see it all along, but I wouldn't let myself believe it. I'm the fool here. The crazy, stupid fool."

"And what if you were right, Sophie? What if I was the kind of guy who was capable of dispatching another man to wherever, whatever Alex has gone to? Don't you think that if you had concerns you should have taken them to the police and not embarked on some ill-advised personal investigation? Didn't you think that you might be putting yourself at risk, too?"

"Please, Zach, please give me, us, another chance."

Tears shone in her eyes. Tears of genuine regret, he had no doubt. But he couldn't find it in himself to forgive her. Not for believing something as nefarious as him possibly being responsible for another man vanishing from the face of the earth—a man who was not only his friend and business partner, but her boss, as well.

"That first time we made love, you said I could trust you. I believed you, and now you've proven me wrong. Go get dressed, I'll call you a cab," he said flatly.

Sophie took a step toward him, her hand out as if to touch him, but he stepped back, avoiding her.

"Don't," he warned. "I can't be in the same room as you right now. Just…go."

Twelve

Sophie let herself into her apartment just as the sun was beginning to peek its pale-golden face over the horizon. A new day, yet to her it felt like the end of the world. She'd betrayed Zach's trust in the worst way possible.

Her apartment looked just the same as it always did, yet Sophie knew without doubt that everything inside her had changed. She'd ruined everything. She—who was always so careful, always so considered—had destroyed her chance at happiness with a wonderful and worthy man. It was one thing to plot, however far-fetched it was, with Mia over lunch, and another thing entirely to act upon it.

She walked into her bedroom and turned back the bed before methodically unpacking her weekend bag and putting things away, with the exception of her dress, which she put in the hamper for dry cleaning. For once she couldn't take any comfort in mundane activities. Not when it felt as if her heart was breaking in two.

Sophie dragged on a pair of cotton pajamas and crawled into her bed, pulling the covers up over her and blocking out the cheerful light of day. Right now she didn't want to face the world, or anything or anyone within it. She'd made what was probably the worst mistake in her entire life and against every caution she'd given herself, too.

It was midafternoon when she awoke with a bitter taste in her mouth and a heaviness in her chest that made her want to cry out loud. She scrubbed her teeth in the bathroom, then went to the kitchen and poured herself a glass of water before curling up on her couch and staring emptily at the blank television screen.

No matter which way she turned things around in her mind, she'd been in the wrong. Zach had been decent and good and professional every step of the way. *She* had been the one to promulgate the kiss between them after that dinner at Claire's, not him. *She* had been the one to actively entice him and flirt with him in the office in the days afterward, even after pushing him away after their first kiss. *She* had been the one to make that first move, to make love to him, to experience the most incredibly uplifting and fulfilling lovemaking she'd ever had the pleasure to encounter. And she knew why it had been so very special because, somewhere along the line, she'd fallen completely and utterly in love with Zach Lassiter. And she'd been the one to destroy that love with her senseless suspicions and irresponsible behavior.

She lifted a hand to her face and pressed her fingertips tightly to her mouth to hold in the wail of grief that rose from deep inside her.

All her life she'd been the one who fixed things, who made things right by taking the load of others, by organizing the sphere in which she lived. But now she'd done the exact opposite. She'd hurt Zach; she'd pulled apart his trust when he'd so carefully, so cautiously, given it to her.

How could she fix this? Was it something she was even capable of? She doubted it. A man like Zach didn't commit easily, not when he already had so much happening in his life. The fact that he continued to work so hard to save his ex-wife from hurting herself and her family—no matter how blind they remained to her vulnerability—spoke volumes about his character.

Deep down Sophie had always known he was that kind of man. So why had she been so imprudent as to believe he had something sinister to hide? What business had it been of hers?

She owed him a massive apology and she needed to know exactly where they stood. Okay, so she knew he probably wasn't in the frame of mind to accept anything from her right now, but at the very least they still had to work together until this business with Alex was resolved. If she could prove to him that she fully accepted she'd been in the wrong, that she could make it up to him somehow, that she'd be even better at her job than she had been before, then maybe, just maybe, he might consider giving her, them, another chance.

Before she could change her mind, Sophie picked up her phone and dialed Zach's cell. He picked up on the fifth ring and she couldn't help wondering if he'd been prevaricating between answering and letting her go to voicemail. Before he could answer, she began to speak.

"Zach, please, hear me out. I know you probably don't want to talk to me right now—"

"And you'd be right. What is it, Sophie?" he replied, weariness weighting his every word.

"I...I..." The words that had been clear in her mind faded on a swell of insecurity. Silence echoed through the earpiece of her phone, forcing her to fill it. "Zach, do I still have a job?"

"That's a good question," he answered slowly. "You betrayed my trust. In the same position, would you continue to work with someone like that?"

Sophie wrinkled her brow. She could discern nothing from the tone of his voice. Nothing of the boss she'd worked with these past weeks. Nothing of the lover who'd filled her heart and driven her body to heights of pleasure she'd only ever dreamed of. A small sound of pain rose from deep inside her. She'd ruined everything.

"No, I guess I wouldn't. Not without a very good reason, anyway. But Zach, we have good reason to keep working together. Without me there you'll only be able to work at one-third capacity. Even with a temp to help you, between Alex's responsibilities and yours, you'd still be struggling."

She heard him sigh through the phone as her words rang true. Pressing her advantage, she continued.

"I know I deceived you, Zach. I went against everything I know in my heart to do so and I'm more sorry than you'll probably ever understand, but I can't leave you in the lurch at work. Not now. Please, at least let me have another chance there."

"All right, but step one toe out of line and—"

"You won't regret it, Zach, I promise you."

He made a sound, somewhere between a snort and a laugh, before answering. His words, when they came, chilled her to the bone.

"I already do. Every second," he said before severing their connection.

Sophie sank slowly to the floor, the phone still

clutched in her hand. She'd wanted to know where she stood and now she knew.

Sophie had to haul herself into work the next morning. Getting up early wasn't the problem; she'd barely slept a wink all night anyway. No, it was the prospect of seeing the recrimination in Zach's eyes that was the hardest thing to deal with. She knew she couldn't put it off. She, of all people, knew how important it was to face up to things, to keep putting one foot in front of the other, day after day, week after week. Eventually a new normal asserted itself. One you could live with. After all, wasn't that how she and her mother had coped after Susannah had gone to live with her aunt?

Somewhere in the dark hours of the night, Sophie had formed a plan to carry her through today, and if that was successful, it would hopefully see her through the next day, and the next.

"New normal, here I come," she said under her breath as she let herself out of her apartment and walked to her car parked on the side of the building.

By the time she reached the office she'd all but convinced herself she could do this. Right up until the moment she saw Zach's SUV in the office's basement parking lot. Her palms grew sweaty on her steering wheel and she had to concentrate to breathe properly. It would have been so much easier had she been the first to arrive today.

"New normal, remember?" she chided herself in the rearview mirror before alighting from the car and making her way to the elevator.

The main office was still unstaffed and despite the fact they had no idea of what she'd been up to over the weekend, she was grateful she didn't have to run the gauntlet. She knew she looked terrible. Two nights of broken sleep did that to a person. Two very different nights, she thought briefly before assembling her features into an expression she hoped would appear calm and capable and letting herself into the executive suite.

Zach's office door was closed and she could hear voices coming from inside. As she was putting her bag away, she heard his door open and Zach and an older couple came out. Past them she could see another woman sitting by Zach's desk. Zach closed the office door behind him and shook the man's hand, then leaned forward to kiss the woman on the cheek, only to be enveloped in a huge hug before, on a strangled sob, she reached for her husband and they walked straight out without so much as acknowledging her.

Zach's face looked strained. It didn't look as if he'd had any more sleep than Sophie had, she realized as he turned and went back into his office, closing the door once again.

There had been something vaguely familiar about the woman who'd left. She wondered if she should offer Zach and the person she'd seen still sitting in his office a hot drink. She supposed if she was going to break the ice between her and Zach, it would certainly be easier to do it with another person there to act as a buffer.

She put her coffee mug on her desk and walked the short distance to Zach's door, knocking sharply before twisting the knob and opening the door.

"Good morning," she said as smoothly as she could. "I wondered if you and your guest would like coffee or tea? Or perhaps some water?"

"Coffee, thanks," Zach bit out crisply. "Anna?"

Sophie felt a frozen chunk of lead settle in the pit of her stomach. This was Zach's ex-wife? Oh, Lord, she didn't know if she was ready for this. Coming face-to-face with the woman he'd chosen to marry, the woman who'd borne his son. The woman who so needed him now that he'd moved heaven and earth to do what he could to help her.

"Just water, thanks," the other woman said, her voice wobbly as if she was crying.

Sophie turned to her with a smile. "Sure thing, I'll be back in a mom—"

Her heart shuddered to a halt in her chest. The walls of Zach's spacious office began to close in on her. Too afraid to speak, to even draw a breath, Sophie straightened and walked out of the office, shutting the door behind her and leaning against its solid surface as if that was the only thing keeping her upright at this point in time.

No wonder the woman who'd just left looked vaguely familiar. The last time Sophie had seen her was twenty-two years ago. The day her sister had left the small rented apartment she'd shared with Sophie and their mother. The day Sophie, in her six-year-old innocence, had believed her four-year-old sister was going for a vacation with her daddy's sister. A vacation? It had been a lifetime. She could still see her baby sister waving excitedly as she was led away by her aunt. Sophie hadn't been able to understand why her mother was sobbing quietly in her bedroom when Suzie was going to come back soon, wasn't she?

It had been several weeks before her mother could even tell Sophie the truth. By then, her mother had become a brittle shell, even worse than she'd been after burying her second husband. It was as if, with Suzie gone, all the light had gone from her world, leaving Sophie to pick up the pieces of the life they'd had before. A simple life, certainly not one with any extravagances in it, but they'd had love. Six-year-old Sophie had made it her mission to show her mother every day that it would be all right, that they still had one another, that they could cope with the gaping hole in their lives where Suzie had been.

Suzie. *Anna Lassiter was Suzie.*

Sure, she'd grown up, she'd changed, and obviously her name had been changed, but Sophie would have recognized her little sister anywhere. The knowledge slowly seeped into her mind, spreading through her body with something akin to hope. But that hope was brought to an uncompromising end when she remembered exactly who Suzie was now.

Zach's ex-wife. An ex-wife she knew he still spoke to almost daily. An ex-wife he still felt duty bound to care for, and Anna desperately needed care if what Zach had told her over the weekend was true.

Sophie pushed off the door and went quickly to the kitchenette, automatically going through the motions of pouring Zach's coffee and a glass of ice water for Anna, complete with a slice of lemon. She put the drinks on a small tray and closed her eyes a moment, drawing in a stabilizing breath before she went back to his office and knocked on the door and let herself in.

She fought the urge to say something to her sister, to beg her to look her in the eyes and recognize what they had lost when they had been split apart all those long years ago. Her hand shook slightly as she put the water glass on a coaster on the edge of Zach's desk, beside where Anna was sitting. She took the opportunity for an assessing glance at the woman little Suzie had become.

It broke Sophie's heart to see the person sitting slightly hunched over in the chair, her blond hair long and stringy—desperately in need of a decent wash and style—her blue eyes, a legacy from her father, dull and filled with misery. She was far too thin, her clothes hanging off her shoulders. Sophie ached to put her arms around her, to try to assure her sister that everything would now be okay, but she didn't have that right.

Suzie was gone. *Anna* sat in the chair here in Zach's office. Anna who'd grown up with another life, another world, a husband, a child—the loss of that child. Sophie felt that loss now, as immediate and as sharp as if she'd experienced it herself.

"Sophie?"

Zach's voice reminded her of her task, of where she was.

"Oh, um, I'm sorry. Here's your coffee. Will there be anything else?"

She met his eyes for the first time since he'd sent her packing from his home, from his bed. She expected to see something there, some flicker or spark, but his gaze remained inscrutable, devoid of any feeling—for her, at least.

"No, thank you. Anna and I will be leaving shortly. I don't expect to be back in the office today and I'd like you to take care of my calls for me."

"Certainly," she said, taking refuge in her old persona. The superefficient executive assistant who never put a foot wrong. The one who hadn't been disloyal to her boss by suspecting him of being party to a heinous crime. The one who hadn't fallen irrevocably in love with him. "It was nice to meet you, Mrs. Lassiter."

The other woman didn't even acknowledge her and continued to sit, staring down at her hands, a slow, steady trail of tears rolling down her cheeks.

Sophie collected the empty tray and left the office,

her legs working automatically, her heart beating so hard in her chest she was surprised Zach and Anna hadn't heard it. In the kitchenette she bent to stow the tray in its cupboard then stood, unmoving, as if not knowing what to do next.

And she didn't know. Not in all honesty. She'd waited all this time to be with her sister again, yet now, having discovered who and where she was, there was no way she could land her discovery on the poor creature in Zach's office.

At least Suzie—no, Anna, she scolded herself—had Zach on her side, Sophie consoled herself as she felt the burning-hot sting of tears in her own eyes. The fact he had her right here, that he'd spent so much time in the past month or so trying to find help and that he'd apparently now convinced her parents—her adoptive parents—to support him in his quest to get treatment for Anna, spoke volumes as to how much he must still love his ex-wife.

Acknowledging the truth of that love was both a blessing and heartrendingly painful. A blessing because now, hopefully, her sister would have the chance to get well again, to be whole. To learn to accept her grief without allowing it to consume her very reason for continuing to live. The pain came in accepting that no matter how much Sophie loved Zach, no matter what chance she'd ever stood of maybe earning his forgiveness for letting him down the way she had, he wasn't hers to love. Never had been, never could be—not when he still loved Anna and when Anna needed him so much.

There was no light at the end of her tunnel. No hope. Even if, by some unexpected and unbelievable twist of fate, Sophie did receive Zach's forgiveness, she could never do that to her little sister.

Anna needed help, pure and simple. It started with Zach and the doctor he'd been consulting with at the Philmore Clinic, and maybe one day it could end with Sophie. She'd been incapable of helping her sister before today but there had to be something Sophie could do for Anna—even if it meant giving up the man she loved with all her heart.

Thirteen

Around visits to the Philmore Clinic, Zach poured himself into his work. It should have been a panacea, but what relief was it when each day he came face-to-face with the woman who invaded his every sleeping moment and most of his waking ones, too?

He hadn't known how Sophie would react at the office the first Monday they were back, but she'd behaved with her old consummate professionalism—her clothing tasteful and not in any way revealing, although with how thoroughly and intimately he knew her now, it didn't take any stretch of the imagination before his body was aching and seething with frustration. If only it could be as simple as just keeping it physical, but what had begun to grow between them had been more than that. At least he'd begun to think so. Foolishly, it seemed—and that was why the discovery of what she'd believed him capable of was even more agonizing. And although Sophie kept her physical distance during the times they had to occupy space together in the office, as intangible as it was, he still *felt* her with him.

The only good thing about the past week and a half was that Anna had finally agreed, with her parents' blessing, to be admitted to the Philmore Clinic and was actively participating in her rehabilitation. Even so, Zach experienced a clutch of fear in his gut each time his cell phone rang. What if she decided to leave, decided that she didn't need Dr. Philmore's treatment any longer? Or worse, that she felt well enough to leave long before she'd been medically cleared? It was a secure facility, but the choice to remain there was hers alone.

He could only hope as each day passed that she could see the good the clinic could do for her and find the strength from somewhere to battle back to the woman she used to be.

At work, though, there was a new tension in the air. Understandable, given the circumstances, but no less comfortable to live and work with. Sophie had been professionalism incarnate, keeping their interactions brief and to the point. Even so, he still felt uncomfortable around her, his mind plagued with memories of the intimacies they'd shared and of the shock of finding out she'd duped him all along. Added to that, the police had recently confirmed there were no new leads as to what the hell had happened to Alex. Some of their clients had grown antsy and Zach had spent a good portion of the week soothing the more volatile among them and talking them down from wanting to take their investment capital elsewhere. He hadn't been a hundred percent successful and that failure rankled him.

He was mentally exhausted by the time he drove home toward the end of the week, wanting nothing more than a scotch on the rocks and a good movie, but tonight he was expected at his first official TCC members' meeting. He could only hope that nothing contentious sprang up to make the meeting take longer than absolutely necessary. After all, per the agenda he'd been emailed earlier in the week, they were to discuss hiring a child-care-center manager. How contentious could that get?

It didn't take long to figure that one out, Zach discovered a couple of hours later.

"I still say it's outrageous that we're even contemplating the need for this here appointment of a center manager," Beau Hacket said, his color rising in his face in step with the volume of his voice. "Waste of club funds, in my opinion. What's wrong with a roster of parent helpers?"

"Beau," past president Brad Price said wearily from his position as chairman of the meeting, "stop hashing over something that's a done deal. The child-care center is happening, voted and agreed upon, whether you like it or not, and it will be a professionally run and certified entity in its own right. The appointment of a suitable and qualified manager is an integral part of that process."

"I don't like it and I don't mind telling anybody that," the older man blustered.

"So we've heard," came a wry voice from the back of the room.

Zach couldn't be sure who had said it, but the round of suppressed laughter through the meeting room that followed suggested there were several there who were totally over Hacket's old-school views.

One of the other older members stood up. "I still don't see why this is even an agenda issue."

"That's right," interjected Beau. "What difference does it make who runs the dang thing? It'll be nothing but a hyped-up babysitter service for women who ought to be looking after their babies at home anyway."

Zach could see Brad's wife, Abigail, starting to get hot under the collar. She'd held her peace up until now, but the old man had just pushed one too many buttons.

"Now just one minute—" she started angrily as her husband banged his gavel on the table.

Zach got to his feet and put up his hand. He could hear the others in the room shift in their seats as he did so—some curious as to why he'd stood to speak, others clearly just wishing the meeting would get over and done with.

"I think we need to look at this item calmly and carefully. What has been proposed is clearly far more than a babysitting service, don't you all agree?" He looked around the room, meeting the eyes of those who were clearly on his side as well as a few who weren't.

He continued. "We're talking about child care. Your *children's* care. Your *grandchildren's* care. This isn't just some short-term setup so your wives can enjoy a game of tennis or two on those new courts while your kids are cared for by some glorified nanny. There are enough of you who already have one of those, right?" A smattering of laughter, this time more of camaraderie than ridicule, filled the room. "This is to be a place where your children and grandchildren can learn to be worthwhile people, where they can learn to socialize and interact with other kids and their caretakers in a safe, happy and healthy environment. Where they can learn and grow and allow their parents the time they too need to be worthy citizens of Royal, doing the works they do to make our town great. It would be narrow-minded and shortsighted not to realize that the appointment of a suitable manager is paramount."

He turned and faced Beau Hacket outright. As the old man was the powerful and respected ringleader of the members who'd been most vocal in their disapproval, Zach knew he had to get Hacket onboard if they were to avoid further trouble down the line.

"Mr. Hacket, your daughter has brought new business and capital to our town with her work, work that will hopefully stand Royal in good stead for future movie locations. After all, look at what *Lord of the Rings* did for New Zealand. Why wouldn't we want a piece of that?" Zach could feel the mood in the room beginning to lighten, the tide beginning to turn. "Now she's expecting a family—twins, I'm told. Should Lila put all her hard work—work I'm also told you're incredibly proud of—on a back burner, perhaps never to be touched again, simply because there is nowhere suitable for your grandchildren to be cared for? Don't your grandchildren deserve the very best?"

Beau Hacket spoke gruffly. "Of course they do. But that's why they should be cared for by their mother, at home."

"But what if caring for her babies isn't the best thing for Lila? What if her work is so important to her, so vital to her happiness, that a few hours a week in a center such as we're creating gives your daughter the best of both worlds? Can't you see now how important it is that we consider carefully each and every application so that when an appointment is made we can all be secure in the knowledge that we've found the very best person for the job? For our children, and our grandchildren?"

"He makes a good point, Beau. You don't want any old biddy in charge of our kids," commented the gentleman who'd supported Beau Hacket earlier. "I know I don't want my grandbabies in the hands of some random stranger."

Zach could feel the mood in the room shift, becoming less combative, less old-school versus new.

"Why are you so all-fired keen on this idea, Lassiter? You're not even married," someone yelled from the back of the room.

"No, I'm not. But one day I'd like to think I'll marry again, and have a family of my own—" *again,* he added silently "—and I'd like to think that my wife and I would have a choice about where our children will receive their early learning. I'd like it to be somewhere like here, within the TCC. In a child-care center that embraces the same values that we've all sworn to uphold."

Zach sat down again, satisfied he'd said his piece and satisfied that he'd been heard. As the discussion continued around him, and he fielded the occasional pat on his shoulder or sidelong comment of "Well said" and "Bravo," he began to feel the acceptance of his peers within the TCC. While no one had been overtly unfriendly to him as his membership was under consideration, it seemed that any barriers left between him and the other members had fallen on the heels of what he'd had to say. As the meeting drew to a close, Sam Gordon, Lila Hacket's fiancé, approached.

"Well said, Lassiter. You've given me something to think about, thank you. Can I buy you a drink at the bar?"

And there it was, that sense of acceptance. That sense that no matter his background, no matter what he might have done before, here, at the TCC, Zach was a valued and accepted member.

"Thanks, I'd like that, and call me Zach," he accepted with a shake of the other man's hand. "Everything sorted out for your wedding this weekend?"

Sam put both hands up in the air in a gesture of surrender. "It's all out of my hands and that's the way I'm keeping it. I'm just glad I finally got her to agree to marry me."

By the time Zach returned home that night, Sam Gordon hadn't been the only one offering to buy him a drink. In fact, if he'd taken them all up, he'd have been blind drunk in a cab by now, he thought ruefully as he rolled his Cadillac into its space in his multicar garage. Not ready for bed yet, Zach went through to his den, where he threw himself on the sofa and loosened his tie. All in all, today had been a good day.

He picked up the TV remote and started to surf through the channels, but nothing caught his eye. Instead he muted the TV and just sat for a moment, absorbing the quiet that surrounded him.

Normally he didn't mind being on his own. In fact, by the time his day staff had left the house, he relished it at the end of a hard day. He thought back to the meeting, to how the members had listened to him, allowed him to take charge of the issue, and he realized that the feeling it had left him with was one of happiness.

Zach wasn't usually the kind of guy to dwell on his feelings, but tonight he couldn't stop thinking about two things—people, in particular. He knew Alex would have been proud of him tonight. Even though he and his friend had never discussed the child-care center in depth—after all, they were both leading bachelor lifestyles—he had gotten the feeling that Alex was a deeply family-oriented guy. That providing the best for children was as intrinsic to him as turning the best deal or finding the best investors to make that deal happen.

He missed his friend with a physical ache. Missed their late-afternoon debriefings over a beer in the office after everyone else had gone home for the night.

"Where are you, buddy?" he asked out loud, wishing with all his might that somehow, some way, he'd get the answer he wanted.

The only person in the world who could possibly understand how much he missed his friend was Sophie. Just thinking about her gave him a pang in his chest and he realized, despite seeing her each day in the office, that he missed her and what they'd begun to share together just as much as he missed Alex.

Two people absent from his life. Two things that if set to rights could make him feel wholeheartedly happy again.

Could he set to rights the emptiness that now existed between him and Sophie? Did he even want to try? He weighed the pros and cons in his mind, first examining in depth the hurt he'd felt when he'd found her here, in his den, snooping in his private email. Even now he still tasted the anger that had flooded his entire body when she'd admitted why she'd been poking around. The sense of having been taken for a fool, *used,* by her as she continued with her duplicity.

He'd thought she had genuine feelings for him, had known he was developing them for her. God only knew how long he'd kept her at arm's length, kept his own desires under lock and key. After Anna, he'd been wary of commencing a new relationship. Then, when the feelings between him and Sophie had swelled to the boiling point, it was no wonder they'd spilled over and combusted the way they had.

The way she'd behaved still had the power to rile him up but, he asked himself for the very first time, if the tables had been turned, if he'd suspected she had information about this business with Alex, what would he have done?

Whatever he could.

The answer echoed in his mind. In reality, Sophie had done no more or less than he would have done in the same situation. The only problem had been that she'd discovered things about his personal life that he'd have preferred, out of respect for Anna and her parents, to keep private.

So why had he been so worried about that? Sophie had proven herself to be nothing but the soul of discretion the whole time she'd worked alongside him. Even now, in the face of what had happened between them—with both the highs and lows of what they'd gone through together—she had kept her counsel. She behaved as if nothing had ever transpired between them, as if the status quo had never been ruffled. As if they had never had the wildest sex he'd enjoyed in a long time on the surface of his desk.

Need punched deep and low in his gut. He missed her, all right. Missed what they'd begun to share, missed what they could have continued to share if only he hadn't caught her on his laptop that night. If only he had remained rational in the face of her accusations. If only he hadn't all but banished her from his private life.

It had been the intensity of his protectiveness toward that privacy that he'd reacted to. He could see that now. By keeping Anna and her problems, *his* problems, secured within a box, he hadn't had to face his own feelings about what she was going through—or, more importantly, his own grief.

Zach stood and reached into his back trouser pocket for his wallet and opened it. There, behind a plastic shield, was a photo of Blake, taken shortly before the accident that had claimed his son's life. An accident he, in all honesty, blamed himself for as much as he blamed Anna. If he'd been any kind of husband to her, any decent kind of father, he would have been home that night instead of working late in an attempt to earn a partnership in her father's investment firm.

What had it all been for, he wondered. After the accident, what was left of their marriage had disintegrated—exposed for the empty, guilt-ridden sham it had been from the start. Zach had resigned his position with Anna's father's firm and struck out on his own, quickly getting a reputation for taking risks that paid off, risks that drew Alex Santiago's attention and his offer of a partnership that had quickly led to a strong friendship based on mutual respect.

He dragged his mind away from his missing friend and back to the woman who linked them. The woman who'd been as concerned as Zach about where Alex was. The woman who'd been prepared to do whatever it took to find out. Could he forgive her for not trusting him, for not trusting herself to even approach him about her concerns?

Of course he could. Sophie was good from the tip of her shining golden head to the soles of her delectable feet. Good in a way he had rarely seen outside of his own parents and good in a way he'd almost forgotten existed within the world he'd chosen to inhabit.

Could he forgive Sophie for what she'd done? Of course he could. In fact, how could he not when he'd already admitted to himself that he would have done exactly the same thing to find information if the tables had been turned?

She was hurting inside just as much as he was, he knew it. He'd caught her gaze upon him several times this past week before she'd rapidly averted it and continued with whatever she'd been doing. But within those beautiful, soft brown eyes he'd seen the longing mixed with pain and regret. He wanted to erase that hurt. Ease that longing.

He wanted Sophie Beldon.

Fourteen

The only good thing about getting to the end of this interminable week, Sophie thought, was being able to look forward to Lila and Sam's wedding over the weekend. How Lila and her mother had managed to pull something as important as this together in three weeks defied even Sophie's normally logical and practical mind. They were keeping things small, which made it a great deal more manageable to host at the Double H.

They couldn't want for a more beautiful setting than the Double H. No matter what anyone said about Beau Hacket, or how stuck in the Dark Ages he appeared to be with regard to a woman's place in the world, he had worked hard to build a very special home for his family.

She turned her attention away from the wedding and back to the report she was finalizing for Zach. She'd barely seen him today, but a tiny knot of tension in her stomach reminded her he was due any moment.

He'd been visiting the Philmore Clinic again. She was burning to ask him how Anna was doing, but given how strained the atmosphere was between the two of them, she had no idea where to start. A call to the clinic hadn't elicited any information, either, and had earned a terse remark regarding patient confidentiality. She'd even toyed with phoning Anna's aunt, except she still had no idea what name the woman went by now and had taken that particular frustration out on the private investigator she'd engaged, and now fired. How difficult should it have been for them, with all their resources, to discover that Anna's aunt had married—that Anna's surname had changed and her first name had also been shortened?

Her goal, though, had been reached. She had found her sister, for all the good that it did her.

Sophie's mother had been over the moon with joy when she had phoned her with the news that she'd found Suzie, but she'd been understandably upset and concerned when Sophie told her how ill her sister was. Sophie had briefly toyed with not telling her mom about Anna's mental collapse, worried it might raise old demons of guilt that stemmed from letting her daughter go in the first place, but her mother had been stronger than she'd expected and had coped remarkably well with the news. Even now she and Jim were driving their RV back to Royal from the Reagan Library in California, putting their vacation plans on hold indefinitely. Sophie would be glad of their support but until they got here she was on her own.

Sophie looked up as Zach entered the executive suite.

"Any messages?" he asked.

"Nothing today. I guess everyone's busy getting ready for the wedding tomorrow."

"About that, do you have a plus one on your invitation?"

"Y-yes, I do," she answered hesitantly.

Why on earth would he want to know that? She knew he had received his own invitation, one that had arrived by special delivery this morning.

"And? Are you taking anyone with you?"

"No, I'm going on my own," she said, her spine stiffening in reaction.

"Seems silly for us to take two cars. Why don't I pick you up about three, we can go together?"

She stood there stunned into silence.

"What?" he asked. "You don't think that's a good idea?"

"I'm just confused, is all. Especially after..."

"I'll pick you up at three," he reiterated. "Now, if there's nothing else that's urgent today, we may as well finish up for the week."

Sophie didn't need to be told twice. She'd booked an appointment at Saint Tropez, the upscale spa and hair salon in town, for early tomorrow morning. *Me and half of the invited wedding guests,* she'd thought when she'd been forced to accept an early-morning appointment. Now she was glad she'd gone ahead with it. If she was to spend any time in Zach's company at the wedding, she'd need the armor of perfect hair, face and nails. All the better to claw him with? She almost laughed out loud at the thought. As if she'd ever get that close to him again.

Tears stung Sophie's eyes as she watched Lila and Sam walk together down the aisle toward the celebrant. They'd decided to forgo attendants and the usual traditions, saying they came to this marriage together and that's exactly how they wanted it. Their vows were simple and poignant, each one a very personal testament to the love they shared and the promises they now made to each other. Their shared joy shone through their voices and their eyes, eyes they could barely take off one another throughout the short ceremony.

A gentle breeze blew softly against the bride's diaphanous strapless gown, exposing the soft roundness of her early pregnancy as if with a loving caress. And when the bride and groom kissed, there was an uproar from the crowd as congratulations, whistles and applause filled the air. Finally united as man and wife, they turned to face the gathering, their happiness beaming over everyone present.

While Sophie wished her friend all of the very best, she couldn't help but feel a chasm opening between their lives. Lila was married now, with a family on the way and with a bright successful career. Before, Sophie had barely felt the difference between herself and her married friends, but today in particular created a wistful ache deep in her chest. She was no closer now to long-term happiness than she'd been five years ago, than she'd maybe even be in another five years. It was an incredibly painful truth, and hard to bear—even more so watching Lila's wedding while the man Sophie loved with all her heart, but whom she could never have, stood at her side.

Sophie felt a gentle nudge against her arm.

"Here," Zach said softly.

She looked down, surprised to see a crisply ironed white handkerchief in his hand. She touched a hand to her cheek, surprised to find the tears she'd thought she'd contained liberally running down her face—no doubt ruining the makeup applied so carefully at Saint Tropez that morning.

"Thanks," she said, her voice husky, and dabbed carefully at her eyes and cheeks.

"It was a beautiful ceremony," he said simply.

"Yes, it was. Perfect." Her voice closed on a hitch. "Ex-excuse me, please."

She couldn't bear it a second longer; she needed a moment or two to herself. Without waiting for Zach's response, Sophie turned and pushed her way through the well-wishers crowded around the happy couple and made for one of the guest bathrooms inside the main house. Once inside, she locked the door firmly behind her. She leaned against the solid wood, dropping her head back and closing her eyes, now acutely aware of the hot, inexorable slide of tears down her cheeks.

Pull it together, she told herself sharply. *You're happy for Sam and Lila. Thrilled that they've pulled the threads of their attraction together into a tightly woven future.* And she was truly happy for them—just insanely miserable for herself.

She pushed off the door, opened her eyes and stepped up to the cream marble vanity unit, turning on the cold tap with a vicious twist before thrusting her hands under the cool, gushing water. As it poured over her wrists, she began to calm down, get control of the crazy emotions that ran rampant through her body.

So she'd failed with Zach. She'd abused his trust and she'd failed, coming up with a big fat zero. She could overcome this. There was nothing keeping her in Royal, not now with her mom happily remarried and enjoying her retirement traveling around the country in a luxury RV. She could relocate, find another job somewhere else. Maybe even in Midland. No one said she had to stay in Maverick County. Maybe she could travel farther afield to Dallas or Houston, or even out of state. Her savings and her skills could travel with her and she'd proven over and over again while she was growing up that she could pretty much make a home anywhere.

But what about Anna? a little voice deep inside her asked. *Now you've found her, do you really want to go away?*

Sophie met her gaze in her reflection in the gilt-edged mirror. Could she honestly do it? Could she walk away from the sister she'd been searching for? The sister she'd missed from her life for the past twenty-two years?

No. She couldn't walk away now. Even if she couldn't tell Anna who she was right now, eventually she'd be well enough and Sophie wanted to be there when that happened—for both their sakes. She was just going to have to suck it up, plaster over her broken heart and keep on going. Besides, she couldn't let Alex down now, wherever he was.

Matter-of-factly, Sophie opened her clutch and took out her lipstick and powder. There wasn't much she could do to repair her eye makeup, but thankfully the reception was outdoors and she could probably get away with wearing her sunglasses. She did the best she could to repair the ravages of her tears and then straightened in front of the mirror, pulling her shoulders back and meeting herself square in the eye.

"You can do this," she said firmly. "You're strong, you're intelligent, you're in control. You will survive."

She spied Zach's handkerchief on the vanity and shoved it in her clutch. No doubt he'd prefer it returned without the streaks of mascara and foundation that currently marred its pristine whiteness. She'd launder it for him and return it on Monday.

With one last check in the mirror, Sophie opened the door and walked straight into the last man on earth she expected to see waiting for her.

"I was getting ready to knock the door down. Are you okay?"

"Have you been waiting here all this time?" she asked, incredulous and a little embarrassed.

What if he'd heard her little pep talk to herself in there? She stifled an inner groan of dismay.

"When you didn't immediately come back, I got worried. Then when you didn't come out of the bathroom I began to get even more worried."

"Well, thank you, but you didn't need to bother. I'm fine," she breathed with an insouciance she was far from feeling.

"They're asking everyone to take their seats at the tables. We're together," he said, offering her his arm.

Of course they were seated together, she thought with a tiny sigh. Could today get any worse? She put her hand in the crook of his elbow and tried to ignore the instant flare of heat that burned from her fingertips to the very center of her being. Of course it could, but she'd get through it. She had to.

Fifteen

Sophie's face ached with the effort of keeping a smile plastered on it, but that was nothing compared to the pain in her heart. Every time she'd attempted to create a bit of physical distance between her and Zach, he'd closed it right back up again. It was as if he was doing it on purpose, or as if he didn't trust her to let her out of his sight.

She sighed. It was probably the latter. Although she didn't quite know what he thought she could get up to here. No, she decided. She was just being foolish. The past two weeks had been emotionally taxing and she wasn't her usual self. These stupid, fanciful imaginings were a perfect case in point.

"Dance?" Zach's voice interrupted her thoughts.

"Wh-what?" she asked, momentarily confused.

"I was asking you to dance," he replied with a small quirk of his lips. "It's a common enough custom at weddings, I understand."

"O-of course it is," she stammered.

"So, will you join me on the dance floor?"

He rose and held out a hand to her and with the eyes of several of their clients, who were seated at other tables, upon them, she couldn't very well refuse. She put her hand in his, steeling herself for the reaction she knew was to come, but that was nothing compared to when they joined the swirl of couples on the dance floor. It seemed everyone had decided to join them, which forced them into far closer proximity than was reasonable or comfortable.

Worse, the music had slowed to a dreamy number, one where couples took advantage of the crowded floor to move together hip to hip, their eyes locked on one another, their hands entwined. As beautiful as it was, it was also well-nigh unbearable, Sophie decided as she fought to keep a scant few inches between herself and Zach—a distance that was suddenly closed as another couple bumped into them.

"I'm sorry," Sophie said, pulling slightly away.

The heat of his body had seared through the gown she wore and her hips had brushed all too intimately close to his.

"No problem, but I think you're fighting a losing battle. Why don't you just give in and enjoy it?" he murmured, even as he increased the pressure of his hand against the small of her back, drawing her against him.

Their closeness was both an exquisite pleasure and an excruciating agony at the same time. Her body recognized his instantly, her blood heating and her pulse increasing as they moved together in time to the music. Hip to hip, belly to belly, it was an intoxicating temptation and a cruel torment. Sophie was aware of every flex of muscle, every breath he took.

His light cologne, boosted on the scent of his skin, teased her nostrils and the warm clasp of his hand holding hers made her all too aware of the memory of what that hand had felt like on other parts of her body. Parts that were now taut and aching for more. She stood it for about two minutes, but even that was two minutes more than enough.

"I can't do this," she said abruptly, pulling out of his grasp. Turning away, she made her way through the throng and back to their table.

Zach was instantly by her side. Typical, she thought bitterly. Why give her a few minutes to pull herself together when he could just prolong the torture?

"Come on," he said. "I'll take you home."

"No, I'm fine. Besides, it'd be rude to leave before Lila and Sam do."

He looked at her, a small frown of concern marring his broad forehead.

"Are you sure?"

She painted on a smile. "Of course I'm sure. Oh, look, I've just seen someone I need to catch up with. Will you excuse me?"

Sophie slipped away and began walking toward the opposite side of the festivities. She felt Zach's burning gaze on a spot between her shoulder blades for about the first twenty steps then, mercifully, it was gone. Her shoulders slumped in relief. Having to work with Zach all week was one thing, but having to spend time with him socially, as well—well, that was about more than any woman should be asked to bear.

Circulating among Lila's friends wouldn't normally have been a problem, but Sophie was beginning to feel as if she was playing a sophisticated game of tag by the time Lila was getting ready to toss her bouquet. She'd moved from one group to another, each time shadowed only a few minutes later by Zach. It was exhausting trying to stay ahead of him. Thankfully she could leave soon.

Amid much cajoling and friendly rivalry, she joined the single ladies in a group, waiting for Lila to throw her flowers. She hung well to the back, not at all eager to win the prize. She already knew that she couldn't be with the man she wanted, and no bouquet would magically change that fact—more was the pity.

"Are you all ready?" Lila called out to the group with a beaming smile.

A chorus of voices assured her it was time to hurry up and get on with it. With another smile Lila turned her back and her arm swung in a graceful arc upward, releasing the flowers to fly through the air. Sophie didn't want to catch it, she really didn't. She didn't even so much as have her hands up, but fate had a seriously sick sense of humor right now because sure enough, the flowers sailed directly toward her and would have struck her full in the chest if she hadn't put up her hands to catch them.

For the briefest moment she clutched them to her chest, inhaling the sweet, rich scent of the pale-pink roses interspersed through lush white chrysanthemums, before thrusting them back out and away from her.

"Here," she said to Piper Kindred, who'd been a year ahead of her at school. "You have them."

Before Piper could respond, Sophie thrust the flowers in her hands and turned to walk swiftly away.

"But you won them, fair and square," the curly redhead called out to her retreating form.

"They're all yours," Sophie threw over her shoulder before making her way to her table and collecting her clutch.

She couldn't wait to get out of here and she counted the minutes until Lila and Sam made their goodbyes to everyone. As the departing couple reached her, Sophie put her arms out to her friend and gave her an enormous hug.

"Be happy," she whispered in Lila's ear.

"Oh, I am," her friend answered with a squeeze. "Your turn next. Don't think it won't happen just because you off-loaded the bouquet to someone else."

Sophie forced a smile to her face as she pulled away from Lila's embrace, allowing her to move on to the next person. Then, in a flurry of rose petals, the newlyweds were driven away—a "Just Married" sign in the back window and tin cans clanking the full length of the Double H driveway and lending a slightly incongruous note to the gleaming black stretch limousine Beau had arranged for his daughter and her new husband.

Zach moved beside her.

"Okay?" he asked, his eyes searching hers as if looking for something.

"Yes, I'm fine, although I am rather tired. I'd like to go now but please, do stay if you want to. I'll get a ride with someone else heading back to town."

She gestured in the direction of a small group of people heading toward their cars.

"You came with me," Zach said firmly, "so I'll see you safely home."

The drive back to her house was a long and silent one and when they pulled up outside her apartment, Sophie all but shot out of the car.

"Thank you," she said through the open door. "I'll see you at work on Monday."

She pushed the door closed with a solid thunk and started up the path as fast as her high heels could carry her.

"Sophie, wait!" Zach called out.

She turned and swallowed hard as she saw him striding determinedly toward her.

"Could I come in for a minute?"

Refusal hovered on the tip of her tongue but good manners prevailed. "Sure," she said slightly ungraciously.

Good manners were one thing but she didn't have to sound happy about it. Her hand shook slightly as she tried to insert her key in the door and she startled as Zach's hand closed around hers, guiding the metal key into the keyhole.

"Thank you," she muttered grimly as the door swung open.

He followed her inside, altogether too closely for her equilibrium. She gestured for him to take a seat while she went through to her bedroom and tossed her clutch onto the bed, taking a moment to drag in a steadying breath. Composed again, she went back to the living room.

"Can I offer you something to drink? Tea, coffee, something stronger?" she said as brightly as she could manage.

"Whiskey and water, thanks."

Zach watched as Sophie went to her compact kitchen and he could hear her opening and closing cupboards, then the sound of liquid pouring. She came back through with one glass on a tray together with a small matching jug, its cut crystal cloudy with ice water.

"You're not joining me in a drink?"

"No," she answered matter-of-factly before perching on the edge of the seat farthest from him.

He added water to his whiskey and took an appreciative sip. "Thank you. This is good."

"You're welcome. Are you sure you will be safe to drive home after that?"

"Why? Worried you might be forced to allow me to stay?" he teased.

From the rigid set of her posture, his comment didn't go down at all well. He sighed softly and put his glass down on a coaster.

"Don't worry, Sophie. I'll be fine. I stuck to club soda at the wedding."

"Good," she said abruptly, then frowned. "Although I would have called you a cab."

Zach let loose with a full-bellied laugh, earning a look of censure from his hostess.

"I'm sorry, Sophie. I shouldn't have teased you. Not about that. Seriously, though, I wanted to talk to you tonight."

She stiffened and braced her shoulders, as if expecting bad news. "Really? Nothing that could wait until Monday?"

"No, I didn't want to discuss this at work. I've been thinking a great deal about our last night together." A great deal? Who was he kidding? He hadn't been able to get it out of his mind. He couldn't walk past the windows by the pool without remembering what it had been like to make love to her in the blue water. He'd even considered moving into another bedroom, except he knew he'd never be able to rid himself of the memories they'd created together there, no matter where he did or didn't sleep.

"Oh?" Sophie answered. "I would have thought you'd have managed to move on from that by now."

"I would have, too. But it seems I can't. I can't sleep without dreaming about you, I can't be awake without thinking about you." He shook his head. "Look, I'm going about this all wrong. In fact, I went about everything all wrong that night when I saw you on my computer."

"I was in the wrong. I shouldn't have—"

"No, wait, let me speak. I overreacted, Sophie, and I'm sorry. I was stressed out about Anna and about Alex, and it made me unreasonably defensive."

"But I had no right to go snooping in your private affairs," she said more strongly.

"Actually, you had every right. You suspected, wrongly, thank God, that I was involved in Alex's disappearance. And yes, I had been cagey at work about what I was doing. It's no wonder you put two and two together and managed to get five or more. Seriously, if I had suspected you of being involved in Alex going missing, I would have done exactly the same thing—probably even less subtly." He shoved a hand through his hair, then reached for his drink and took another sip. "Look, I'm really sorry, Sophie. It's been a hellish time and you bore the brunt of it. What with Anna going missing a few days beforehand and then finally getting her parents to agree she needed help, I just lashed out at the most convenient person."

"Me?"

"Yeah, they say you tend to do that with the ones closest to you." He paused, letting his words sink in a little before he continued. "And I do want to be close to you, Sophie. This past week has taught me that. I'm really sorry I hurt you and that I was so cruel. I hope you can forgive me and, more importantly, that you'll give me, us, another chance. I care for you, I really do, and I think we could make a strong future together. Obviously, Anna will always be a part of our lives—"

"No! Stop!" Sophie held up one hand, shaking her head frantically, her eyes wide open, stark against the paleness of her skin. "Don't, I can't. *We* can't. It's impossible."

Her words cut like razors across his nerves. *Can't? Impossible?* When he spoke he tried to infuse his words with as much persuasion as he possibly could.

"Sophie, please. I have very strong feelings for you, and I'm pretty sure you do for me, too. Can't we at least try to make it work? Don't you think we deserve one more chance?"

Sophie's head dropped and she stared at her hands clenched on her knees. He clearly heard the shuddering breath she drew in before she spoke.

"Zach, please, don't get me wrong. I'm honored that you think you have feelings for me—"

"I don't *think* I do, Sophie. I *know,*" he said with quiet conviction.

He'd expected resistance—it was only natural after the way he'd treated her—but he would wear that resistance down, however much it took to do so.

She lifted her head and looked directly at him, her beautiful eyes swimming with unshed tears. "I can't accept them, Zach. Please respect that."

"Respect what? You're not telling me anything. At least tell me why."

She shook her head just as a tear began to track a silvered trail down one cheek. A tear that just about rent his heart in two.

"Please, Zach, please go. This is painful for me. I need you to leave, now."

There was nothing else for it. She'd asked him to go and while every cell in his body protested, commanding that he stay—comfort her, argue with her, figure out what the hell it was that was keeping her from him—he rose from his chair and saw himself to the door.

Sixteen

Zach sat in his car, still parked at the curb outside Sophie's place. One hand on the wheel, the other poised to turn on the ignition. But he didn't move. All he could do was think about the woman he'd walked away from. It was crazy. He hadn't gotten where he was today by giving up, by simply walking away because someone had asked him to. His entire reputation had been built on taking risks and winning. And he wasn't about to stop doing that now.

Decision made, he flung open his car door and slammed it behind him, keying the remote locking button as he strode back up Sophie's path. He reached the door and, only just resisting the urge to pound on its painted surface and holler at her to let him back in, politely pressed the doorbell.

"Who is it?"

"It's me."

"Zach, I asked you to go. I'm all done talking about this."

He could hear the weary unhappiness in her voice and it made his gut twist.

"And I'm not," he insisted. "I'm also not leaving until you tell me exactly why you're not prepared to give us another chance. The way I see it, we can do this one of two ways. Either I stand here shouting through your door, or you can let me in and we can do this face-to-face."

Silence.

"Sophie—" he pressed the doorbell again "—just how much sleep do you think you're going to get with me doing this every five seconds?"

Slowly the door opened in front of him.

"About as much as I've had all week. Fine, come in then, before you disturb my neighbors."

"Thank you."

He couldn't quite keep the smug satisfaction out of his voice. She'd caved far sooner than he'd have guessed.

"I don't know why you're doing this," she said wearily, wrapping her arms around herself. "I'm entitled to not want to be with you, you know."

"Sure you are, but you really *do* want to be with me, you just won't let yourself. That's different. Here," he said, taking her by her shoulders and gently guiding her down onto one end of the sofa before settling beside her. "Now tell me why you're prepared to let go of what is probably the best thing ever to happen to either of us."

Sophie looked at him and from the expression on her face, it was almost as if doing so caused her immeasurable pain. "I...I don't know where to begin," she said shakily.

"Try the beginning," he coaxed, his hands reaching to hold hers as if to infuse her with the courage she needed to get started.

"You know that my sister was separated from us when we were little. Mom and I started over. Just the two of us for over twenty years. Mom met a really great guy four years ago and she finally remarried. It took her all that time to be willing to take a risk on loving another man again, and she finally had the courage to take what he offered her with both hands. They've been away, fulfilling their dreams of visiting every presidential library around America, and she's finally happy."

Sophie fell silent for a moment, then rose abruptly from her seat to begin pacing the floor.

"Over the years I'd asked Mom about finding Suzie, but it would always make her cry, so I learned to shut up about it—to just tuck it away inside. But then a couple of months ago, Mom asked if I still wanted to find her. We talked about it and decided now was a good time for us to try. To see if we could establish a bond again, if she was willing.

"It hasn't been easy. All the information we had on my stepdad's sister lead to dead ends." Her mouth curved into a rueful twist. "And as you know, my investigative skills aren't up to much. Recently, I hired a private investigator, but that proved to be an exercise in futility. He was either lazy or useless or both," she said bitterly. "And then Suzie just turned up in front of me one day. Just like that."

"Seriously? But that's wonderful news, isn't it?" Zach was even more confused.

While he still didn't see what this had to do with him and Sophie, surely it had to be exactly what she'd hoped for, especially after all this time.

"Yes, and no," Sophie prevaricated.

He could see she was battling with what she had to say. Choosing her words and turning them over in her mind carefully before speaking.

"Explain," he demanded, impatient now to get to the root of what Sophie saw as the problem keeping them apart.

"Suzie's full name was Susannah, and it seems that her aunt changed her name when she adopted her. And it would also seem that she remarried soon after, with Suzie taking her aunt's new surname, as well. Of course, since then, Suzie herself has married and had a child."

Zach started to get a cold prickling feeling down his spine. Suddenly he didn't like where this was heading.

"Zach, Anna Lassiter, your ex-wife, is my sister."

Seventeen

Sophie watched as her words slowly sank in for Zach. Before he could say anything, though, she plowed on with what she knew had to come next.

"It's impossible for us to have another chance. As much as I'm attracted to you—" she closed her eyes briefly, summoning all the courage she could muster "—as much as I love you, I cannot take my sister's chance of happiness and recovery away from her."

Zach got up and put his hands on her shoulders, forcing him to face her.

"Anna and I are good friends, Sophie. Nothing more than that now, and we haven't been anything more for a very long time."

"How can you say that?" she demanded. "You forget I've seen you taking calls from her almost daily for the past eighteen months. I've seen how much you care about her. Can you categorically say that there's no way that when she's better you two won't make a go of your marriage again?"

"Yes, I do care for her, deeply, but not in the way you're thinking. Not as a lover, not as a husband. We're divorced," he said calmly, "and we're staying that way. We found out very early on in our marriage that we were wrong for each other, and we remedied that."

"But she can't live without you, Zach. She needs you like she needs no one else."

He fell silent. Even he couldn't argue with that, she thought painfully. His hands dropped from her shoulders and he turned away from her, one hand reaching up to rub at his face. Sophie went to step forward, to offer him comfort, but she stopped herself just in time. They were at an impasse. An awful and horrible stalemate where another person's very well-being hung in the balance.

"Zach, I'm not going to do anything to upset her world. Not now I've finally found her. I'd like to get to know her again, to be a part of her life, to be her sister. Can you deny me that?"

Zach threw himself back down on the sofa. "This is all such a mess," he said, shaking his head. "You know, when I met her I thought she was cute. Pretty, but not in a stuck-up kind of way, despite her upbringing. Her parents were older and she was a much-cherished daughter. I never knew she wasn't their biological child and she never said anything herself. Do you think she knows?"

Sophie shrugged. Even though it hurt she had to say it. "How much do you remember of your life when you were only four? It's possible that with time she's forgotten all about Mom and me."

"Whether she remembers you guys or not, it may explain why she has always been more emotionally delicate than most people. As if she was afraid that people would abandon her, you know? I never really thought about it much. In fact, that whole vulnerability about her really drew me in. I wanted to be the big strong man for her. I guess I'm still doing that now.

"I worked for her father and I have to admit that when I first met Anna, I did see an opportunity to get a leg up within the company. Initially, at least. When we married, though, I really thought I loved her. At least I'd convinced myself I did. It didn't take long before we both realized we'd made a mistake. We were taking steps to formalize our separation when Anna discovered she was pregnant with Blake."

He sighed again, deeply. "She struggled after the birth. She felt trapped in a marriage neither of us wanted anymore and motherhood didn't come instinctively for her. It didn't help that I was pulling extralong hours at the office because, with Blake's birth, I was offered the promotion I'd wanted. The night of the accident she'd called me at the office, begging me to come home. Threatened to take Blake away from me if I didn't come home right there and then. She was unreasonable and I couldn't calm her over the phone, no matter what I said. It scared me. I headed home as fast as I could but I was already too late.

"Anna has never been able to get over her guilt over what happened. It's eaten her up inside, bringing her to where you saw her the other day."

"Thank you," Sophie said. "Thank you for telling me, for being honest."

"Too many people tried to hide Anna's condition for far too long already, including her parents. They thought—hoped—that all she needed was time, but she needs more than that. The only way she'll ever stand a chance of getting better is if she and the people around her are up front about all of it."

"Her parents finally came around?"

Even though it stuck in Sophie's craw to call them Anna's parents, they had brought her up to the very best of their ability, and she'd seen for herself when they'd left the office last Monday morning just how distraught they were for Anna.

"Reluctantly, but as with everything they do, now that they're on board they're behind her recovery all the way. They've even started organizing a fundraiser back in Midland for the Philmore Clinic." He shook his head with a rueful smile. "You have to hand it to them. They may be late to the party, but they sure know how to arrive."

Sophie couldn't be as magnanimous. "But if they'd stood behind you sooner, Anna wouldn't be in this position."

"Possibly, but we'll never know that. Which, I guess, brings us back to us. Anna and I are not a couple. If anything I'm her best friend, Sophie, that's all. How she'd handle you and me being a couple, well, I guess I'd have to discuss that with her doctor."

Sophie shook her head sadly. "I really want my sister back, and I'm not prepared to do a single thing that might jeopardize that."

"Not even if it means our future happiness? Sophie, I love you. Please, let's work this out."

"I can't," she sobbed, unable to hold back her emotions a second longer. "I just can't."

Zach rose to his feet and reached for her, but she put up both hands and shook her head.

"No, please don't. Don't touch me. Just...please, don't!"

"Okay," he said, his expression somber. "But I'm not giving up."

She couldn't even summon a reply and when the front door closed behind him, she sank to her knees on the carpet and let it all out. All the fear, all the longing she'd had to find her baby sister. All the yearning she'd had for her love for Zach to be returned, only to finally receive it and have it snatched out of her hands by fate.

By Monday morning Sophie was still a mess. She'd barely slept all weekend and getting out of her bed for work had taken the last of her energy. She went through the motions, checking the mail, scanning email, readjusting her schedule accordingly. By midmorning she was beginning to feel almost human again, except for the constant tenterhooks she was on waiting for Zach to show up at the office.

He finally came through the door about midday, looking little better than she did herself. He walked straight up to her desk and stopped in front of her.

"Are you okay?" he asked.

"I'll live," she replied, not bothering to dress up her fractured emotions into anything pretty.

He cracked a small smile. "I'm pleased to hear that. Do you have anything vitally pressing for the rest of the day?"

She shook her head.

"Good," he continued. "Then you'll be able to come with me."

"Come with you? Where?"

"To see Dr. Philmore."

"What? Why?"

"We've been talking. He'd like to meet you."

"But why? Does he think I need help, too?"

Zach let out a short bark of laughter. "No, you goose, of course he doesn't. But he does want to talk to you about Anna. Can you come with me?"

"Of course. When do you want to leave?"

"How about now?"

"Just give me a minute to back up and I'll be ready."

Sophie's shaking hands flew over her keyboard. She was going to meet the doctor who was treating Anna. Did that mean he might even let her see her sister? Lord, she could only hope so.

She felt sick with excitement and trepidation as they drove to the Philmore Clinic. Zach seemed equally tense and reluctant to speak. The clinic was some ways out of Royal, set on sprawling grounds with massive oak trees providing shade across the well-kept lawns.

"It looks more like a country club than a clinic," Sophie remarked as Zach pulled up his SUV in the gravel parking lot.

"Yeah, it has that feel about it, but don't let that fool you. The place is one of the best of its kind. I wouldn't have suggested Anna come here if it wasn't."

"Of course," Sophie agreed, wondering anew just how deeply Zach's feelings ran for his ex-wife.

While his protestations on Saturday night had been very much to the contrary, he seemed prepared to go a great deal further than someone who was simply a good friend. What was she worried about anyway, she asked herself. It wasn't as if she was going to take him up on his offer to pick up where they'd left off. Not now with her sister so obviously dependent on him. It just wouldn't be right.

They ascended the wide, shallow stairs to the front door of the clinic together and Zach held the door for Sophie before following her inside.

A woman greeted them. "Ah, Mr. Lassiter, Dr. Philmore is expecting you in his office. You know the way?"

"Yes, thank you, Betty."

"They seem friendly enough here," Sophie commented nervously.

"They are, and they're devoted to their patients, too."

Sophie tried to ignore the burning sensation in her stomach as Zach guided her along the carpeted hallway before stopping outside a paneled door. He rapped on the surface, then opened the door upon the command of the man inside. She didn't know what she'd been expecting of the doctor, but it wasn't the trim and attractive man who rose to greet them as they entered. He couldn't have been much older than Zach, she thought, maybe mid- to late thirties at most.

His handshake was firm and dry and the warm light in his blue eyes instantly put her at ease as he gestured for them to take a seat in the easy chairs grouped near a bay window overlooking the grounds.

"Thank you for coming, Ms. Beldon," he said, settling himself into one of the chairs. "Can I offer you two anything? Tea? Coffee or a cool drink?"

"No, thank you, I'm fine," Sophie managed through dry lips.

"Same here," answered Zach.

"All right then, I suppose you want to know why I requested that Zach bring you here, so let's cut to the chase. I understand you haven't seen Anna, your sister, for a little over twenty years?" the doctor said smoothly.

"That's right. Twenty-two years, to be exact."

He nodded. "That's some time to be apart. I can see why you'd be anxious to find her. Zach tells me that you recently began searching for her."

Sophie nodded in response.

"Can I ask you why you didn't try earlier?"

She stiffened in her seat. "I beg your pardon?"

Was he implying she should have tried harder? Earlier?

"Please, don't take offense. I'm merely getting the full picture."

"Up until recently my mother was still too unhappy and too fragile herself to instigate a search for my sister. I think finding her earlier would have only reopened old wounds that were already too painful to bear. My mother is remarried now, she's happy. We recently decided, together, to instigate a search for her. We thought if we could find Suzie—Anna—then that might just bring everything full circle, for all of us. Besides which, we needed to know for ourselves that she was okay, that she was happy without us."

Dr. Philmore nodded. "Anna's is a complex case but I think, in part, the complexity comes from her vulnerability in being alienated from you and your mother when she was so young. She obviously had a very strong bond with you both and while she's suppressed many of her early memories, she has begun to talk about you."

"She has? She remembers me?" Sophie sat forward on the edge of her seat.

"She does. More importantly she remembers how safe she felt with you. I think it would be good for you to visit with her, reestablish your contact with one another, get to know one another again."

She couldn't believe it. She'd been worried that with Anna's illness she might have to put off meeting her again, maybe even forever. It had been one of the many things that had plagued her through Saturday night and most of Sunday.

"When can we start?" she asked, eagerly.

"How about now?" the doctor answered with a warm smile.

"Is she in her room?" Zach asked. "Perhaps I should introduce them."

"Yes, and yes, I think that's a great idea. Well," he said, standing up and offering his hand to them both, "it's been lovely meeting you, Ms. Beldon. Always a pleasure, Zach."

As they rode the elevator to the floor where Anna's room was, there were butterflies in Sophie's belly, great big butterflies doing loop-de-loops.

"You'll stay with us, won't you?" she asked Zach as they began to walk down a long, wide corridor.

"As long as you need me to," he promised and took her hand to give it a reassuring squeeze.

Instantly Sophie felt at ease. He did that for her. Thinking about it, he did that for everyone. While he might have built his reputation on being a risk taker, he also had the unerring ability to make people feel secure about his decisions. No wonder Anna depended upon him so much.

"We're here," he said, interrupting her thoughts.

The butterflies zoomed back big-time as Zach knocked on the door and slowly opened it.

Eighteen

"Zach!"

Obvious delight at seeing Zach filled Anna's voice, reminding Sophie of the bond between these two. A bond she could never break, nor did she want to. Sophie hung back slightly behind Zach. This was going to be more difficult than she had anticipated.

The woman who rose to meet them was a far cry from the broken creature Sophie had last seen in Zach's office. Her hair was clean and gleaming, caught back off her beautiful face with a couple of clips. She wore a little makeup, too, which emphasized her blue eyes and the sculpted cheekbones both girls had inherited from their mother.

"I've brought you a visitor today," he said, turning slightly to draw Sophie forward.

Sophie met her sister's gaze, wondering if this time Anna might recognize her. Either way, she decided, it wouldn't matter. They'd make new memories now. Better ones, ones that would take them through the rest of their lives, because Sophie knew to the depths of her soul that she'd never lose hold of her sister ever again.

Anna's brow creased as she looked at her, her eyes suddenly unsure before a new light dawned within their depths.

"Sophie? Is it really you?" Anna said, taking another step forward.

Before Sophie realized it, the two women had closed the gap between them and were in one another's arms.

"Yes," she whispered, her throat thick and her eyes burning with tears of relief and joy. "It's me, at last."

The sound of Zach clearing his throat made them draw apart, but still Anna clutched Sophie's hand as she had so very many years ago.

"I'll leave you two to get reacquainted, okay? Call me when you need me to come and get you, Sophie."

"Thank you," she said softly.

He lifted his chin in acknowledgment. "It was the very least I could do, for you both."

There was something in the tone of his voice that made Sophie take a harder look at him. To look beyond the weariness that painted his features into tight lines, and to the pain that lay behind his eyes. He stared at her, as if willing her to change her mind about them, but she knew she couldn't. Not now. Not when it could hurt her sister, whose psyche was already frail and brittle.

When Zach was gone, Sophie suggested they make the most of the early-fall afternoon and take a walk outside around the grounds. Once outside she linked arms with Anna and began to stroll.

"I never thought I'd see you again," Anna said softly

when they got outside, her voice choking. "Or our mom. Is she...?"

"She's fine. She's due back home any day. She's missed you so much, we both have."

Anna nodded slowly, as if assimilating the words in her mind. "I remember her perfume, her hugs, her smile. I missed them. I used to think that if I was very good I'd be allowed to go home and I tried so very hard, but it never happened."

Sophie's throat tightened again as she battled to hold back tears. Her sister spoke with an air of detachment, as if she was talking about someone else, not the confused four-year-old she had been. She threaded her fingers through Anna's and gave them a gentle squeeze. She had no words. There was nothing she could say that could ever fill the years they had lost. Any bitterness, any ill will she'd ever felt toward Anna's adoptive family had to be put aside and she reminded herself to give thanks for the fact that, despite the past, they had a chance for a new start now.

"She still wears the same fragrance," Sophie eventually managed with a watery smile. "Some things don't change."

"I've changed," Anna answered flatly. "I'm not Suzie anymore."

"I know," Sophie acknowledged with another gentle squeeze. "But you're still my sister and I love you. That will never change."

"You don't know what I did."

Agitation filled Anna's voice. She stopped walking and pulled her hand free from Sophie's clasp. Fine tremors racked her frail form.

"I know." Sophie worked hard to keep her voice level,

reassuring. "I also know you can't keep blaming yourself."

Looking at her sister, Sophie couldn't help but be aware of the massive gulf that lay between them. A gulf created by time and upbringing. By choices they themselves had no say over.

"I'm a monster."

"Anna, you're not a monster. Not by any stretch of the imagination," she hastened to reassure her sister.

"I didn't want him at first," Anna said, assuming that air of detachment she'd had earlier.

Was that how she coped, Sophie wondered, distancing herself from what had happened, from her feelings, until it all became too much and it overwhelmed her again?

"I wanted a termination but Zach wouldn't hear of it. We were already separating, I wanted out of that marriage as much as he did. He changed his mind. He said we could make it work, for the baby's sake. For a while I believed him."

The tremors increased. Alarmed, Sophie guided Anna to sit on a bench beneath one of the spreading oak trees that dotted the expansive lawns. If Anna continued to become upset, she'd need to call for help. Maybe coming outside together hadn't been such a great idea.

"We don't have to talk about this right now," she soothed.

"No," Anna said, her voice suddenly firmer than it had been before. "I need to. I need you to hear it, from me."

"Okay, I'm listening."

"I loved him when he was born, but he terrified me. This tiny baby so dependent on me, and our marriage dependent on him. It was all wrong. So wrong." Anna rubbed her arms, up and down, up and down. "I couldn't cope and I couldn't ask for help. Zach did what he could, but I became such a bitch to live with."

Anna got up suddenly and began to pace, still rubbing her arms, her movements jerky, haphazard. Sophie watched her with concern twisting her gut. Everything in her wanted Anna to stop telling her story, to stop torturing herself like this, but her sister had made it clear she needed to tell it. Sophie could only honor that wish and give her the attention she deserved.

"I drove the car when I shouldn't have, drove too fast on wet roads, and I was angry. Angry at Zach for not being there for me every second of the day, angry at myself for needing him so damn much—angry at Blake for being born. He didn't deserve to bear the brunt of my chaotic emotions, neither of them did.

"Zach and I married for all the wrong reasons. We were destined to fail. I saw Zach as a way out. I knew he wanted to get ahead at my father's firm, so I used him. I convinced myself I loved him and that I would make the best wife in the world. After all, hadn't I been the best daughter for most of my life?"

Anna stopped pacing, stopped rubbing and instead wrapped her arms around herself. Sophie smiled a little, recognizing the very same action she did when she was unsure or unsettled about something.

"Oh, Anna." Sophie got up and put her arms around her sister, trying to absorb the misery and cynicism projecting from her every word.

"No, don't." Anna pushed Sophie away. "Don't make it all right. I have to take responsibility for my part in all this. It's the only way I'll ever get better."

Sophie took a step back. It was a harsh reality, but her sister wasn't the little four-year-old who'd relied upon her for everything anymore. She was a grown woman. A woman who'd completed her education, married, had a child and then seen the death of that child and her marriage. Sophie had concentrated for so long on the young Suzie that she'd completely forgotten to rationalize that she had grown up, become a mature adult. They were contemporaries now, neither needing the care of the other but there for support, for friendship, for love.

"I'm sorry. I can't help wanting to make it all better for you. It's the way I'm wired, I suppose," she said with a small uncomfortable laugh.

Anna stared back at her. "Even after everything I've just said?"

"Especially after everything you have just said," Sophie affirmed. "I'm here for you and our mom will be, too. For as long as you need or want us. I promise."

"Zach said the same thing. He's a good friend. I don't deserve it. Not from him. Not from you. Not any of it." Tears began to track down Anna's face. At first slowly, then faster and faster until she shook with sobs. She didn't object when Sophie put her arms around her again.

"You do," Sophie said firmly. "You deserve our support and our love."

"I just feel so guilty. Not just for what I did, but for what I'm doing now. I'm holding him back. He's so damn noble I know he's putting me ahead of other things in his life, other people. I want him to move on, but I'm too frightened to do this on my own."

"You're not on your own. We'll all be here for you, with you. Trust me, Zach wants you well again, we all do."

She held her sister until the sobs calmed down, until she just gave a tiny hiccup every now and then. Sophie rubbed her sister's back, trying to infuse her love and comfort into Anna's gaunt frame.

"I want to go back inside now," Anna said plaintively.

Sophie tucked her arm around her sister's slender waist and walked her slowly to the main building. She accompanied Anna to her room, settling her in the easy chair near the window that looked out over the gardens.

"Can I get you anything? Call anyone?" she asked, reluctant to leave her.

"No. I just want to think."

"Okay, I'll be going, then."

Sophie got as far as the door before Anna's voice halted her in her tracks. "Will you come back?"

"Sure, every day if you'll have me. And you can call me, too, if you like. Here." Sophie reached into her bag for her notebook and a pen and scratched her details down. "Anytime, okay? If you need me, or just want to talk—call."

"I'd like that."

"Me, too," Sophie said softly, then let herself out of the room.

Downstairs, she phoned Zach and waited outside for him to arrive, replaying her time with Anna over in her head. One thing kept sticking in her mind: Anna's guilt over holding Zach back, together with her adamant statement that she and Zach were just friends. Her feelings about their marriage exactly mirrored what Zach had told her himself. Sophie's head spun. Could she do it? Could she have it all? Could she have a new relationship with her long-lost sister and have the man she loved, as well? In time, could Anna accept that Zach and her big sister were a couple?

She could only hope and pray it was so.

Nineteen

Zach drove carefully back from the clinic, his eyes flicking to Sophie sitting next to him then back to the road ahead. She hadn't said much about her visit with Anna, only that it had been good to see her sister again and that she was looking forward to spending more time with her. He hoped against hope that maybe now she'd begin to see that there was no grand passion between him and his ex-wife—only a friendship based on all they'd been through together.

They pulled up outside Sophie's apartment and he walked her to the door.

"Will you come in?" she asked.

"Sure."

"I'll get us something to drink. What would you like?"

"Just iced water or a soda, thanks."

He watched her as she walked to her kitchen, unable

to tear his eyes off her and biting his tongue hard to prevent himself from bombarding her with questions about her meeting with Anna. She returned with two glasses filled with ice and soda.

"Thank you for taking me to see Anna today," she said as she perched on the seat opposite him.

"You needed to see each other. To reconnect. It's been far too long."

"Yeah, it has. So much has changed."

She sounded wistful. Was that regret in her voice? Had he done the wrong thing?

"You're not sorry you went, are you?"

"No, not at all. I'm just sad for all we've missed out on. We've grown up into such different people."

"You were bound to be different, whether you grew up together or not," he pointed out carefully.

"I know." Sophie shrugged. "But for so long in my mind she's been my baby sister, you know? Someone I had to look out for."

"And now she's all grown up?"

"Yeah, she doesn't need me like she used to."

"She still needs you, Sophie. But as an equal, I think."

She nodded and smiled. "I pretty much came to that conclusion, too. It's a strange thing to have to admit that you're not needed anymore when you've spent your whole life feeling guilty for not being there for someone, for not being able to do more."

"I need you," he said simply. "I love you, Sophie, and I need you in my life like I've never needed anyone before."

"Even after everything I've put you through?"

"After trying to seduce my secrets from me?" he asked. "More than ever. After being my right hand since

Alex went missing? Like you could never know. After working your way into my heart and my mind until all I think about every day, all I want is you? Definitely."

"I don't deserve you."

"Then we don't deserve each other, but who says we have to? Can't we just reach for what we want and love each other, for the rest of our lives? Do you believe me now when I say that Anna and are not in love with one another? Sophie, are you prepared to try again—to put the past behind us and to move on and build a future together?"

His heart hammered in his chest as he waited for her reply. This was the hardest thing he'd ever had to do, this waiting. He'd known after what she'd told him on Saturday night that he'd have to prove to her that he and Anna were not a couple in a romantic sense any longer. That was why he'd spoken with Dr. Philmore and arranged for Sophie to meet with him. Yes, he and Anna would always be friends—you didn't go through what they'd been through without forging some sort of lifelong connection—but that's where they began and ended. The kind of lifelong connection he wanted with Sophie was another bond entirely. It was the kind of bond his parents had, the kind of bond he'd never dreamed he would be lucky enough to have with another person, especially after the disaster of his first marriage.

Now everything lay in Sophie's hands. His heart, his hopes, his future.

"I—I would like to," she said hesitantly, then her voice strengthened and she spoke with more conviction. "But I need to know something first."

"Anything, just ask," he said, hardly daring to hope.

"I can understand your grief over the failure of your marriage with Anna, over what it has cost both of you, especially with losing your son. And I could understand if you never wanted to take that step again, to have a family. I just need you to know that if you're ever ready to be a father again, I want with all my heart to be the one to give you that gift."

Zach moved from his chair to kneel in front of Sophie. He clasped her hands in his and drew them to his lips.

"Sophie, I couldn't imagine a better mother for our children. Will you be my partner in life, in everything that matters to me? Will you marry me?"

She gave him a tremulous smile. "Yes, I love you, Zach. I would be honored to marry you."

"Thank God," he said, pulling her into his arms and closing his lips over hers.

He held her tight to his body, loving the way she fit against him. Two halves of the same whole. She kissed him back with every bit as much fervor as he kissed her, their lips igniting a slow-burning fire between them. A fire he knew, after all they'd been through, nothing could extinguish. Zach pushed his hands through the silken strands of her hair to cup the back of her head as he deepened the kiss, as their tongues stroked and probed, retreated and returned again in a dance that made his blood sing in his veins.

This was right in every way. *She* was right for *him* in every way.

Their clothes seemed to melt from their bodies with the heat of their passion for one another and with each touch, each caress, they rediscovered each other's bodies. Zach rolled onto his back right there on her living room floor and pulled Sophie on top of him. She straddled his hips, her hands tracing circles over his chest, his abdomen and lower.

"I love you, Sophie," he said again as she lifted her hips and positioned her body over his aching arousal.

"I love you, Zach, always," she answered as she slowly accepted him into her body and, he hoped, forever into her heart.

She rocked gently against him and his hands gripped her hips, holding her in place as her hands braced on his chest. She increased her tempo, making his pulse rocket upward in increments. He reached up to palm her breasts, to roll her nipples between his fingertips and squeeze them gently. He could feel the tension building in her body, building in his, and then she tumbled over the edge with a cry, her body reaching its peak and dragging his answering response from deep inside of him.

Their lovemaking had never been more perfect, more in sync. When she collapsed against him, he closed his arms around her and made a silent vow that she would forever be safe in his embrace, that she and any children they were lucky enough to have would always come first in his life, no matter what. He would never make the same mistakes again. This marriage would be based on love, pure and simple—not on duty, not on doing the right thing, unless doing the right thing was loving someone with your heart and soul for the rest of your days.

Much later, after they'd made it to her bed and made love again, they lay in the encroaching darkness just holding one another and Zach admitted he'd never before felt such contentment in his life. Anna would get well again. He and Sophie would build a new life together. There was only one fly left in the ointment. Alex. Where on earth was he?

As if sensing where his thoughts had traveled, Sophie

lifted her head from his chest and met his gaze, tracing the outline of his brow with one finger.

"Problem?"

"Just thinking," he said.

She continued to trace the angles of his face and began to outline his lips with the barest touch. He opened his mouth and caught her finger gently between his teeth, laving it with his tongue. He felt her response as every muscle in her body tightened.

"About Alex?" she asked, gently extricating her finger and leaning up on one elbow.

"How did you know?"

"Because not knowing where he is, that's the only thing that stops the future being perfect right now."

He knew what she meant. It had felt strange accepting the TCC membership without his friend and sponsor by his side, and now he was embarking on marriage with the woman he loved without even knowing where his friend was.

"Zach?"

"Hmm."

"With Anna's recovery still underway and Alex still missing, let's not plan our wedding just yet. We need to be sure that Anna is going to be okay and I know how important your friendship with Alex is. Let's wait until we have some idea if—*when*," she corrected herself firmly, "he's coming back."

"Are you sure?"

"Absolutely. He's your best friend and he means a lot to me, too, both as a boss and a friend. Somehow it doesn't feel right to plan a date until we know more."

Zach pulled Sophie down against him, folding his arms around her. "How did I ever get so lucky as to find you?"

"I'm the lucky one," she argued back, reaching up to kiss him. "I plan to keep reminding you of that for the rest of our lives."

"And I plan to hold you to that." He smiled in return, confident that the future would be a whole lot brighter with her in it.

* * * * *

TEXAS CATTLEMAN'S CLUB:
THE MISSING MOGUL
Don't miss a single story!

RUMOR HAS IT by Maureen Child
DEEP IN A TEXAN'S HEART by Sara Orwig
SOMETHING ABOUT THE BOSS... by Yvonne Lindsay
THE LONE STAR CINDERELLA by Maureen Child
TO TAME A COWBOY by Jules Bennett
IT HAPPENED ONE NIGHT by Kathie DeNosky
BENEATH THE STETSON by Janice Maynard
WHAT A RANCHER WANTS by Sarah M. Anderson
THE TEXAS RENEGADE RETURNS by Charlene Sands

What will happen when this beauty tries to tame the beast?

*Here's a sneak peek at the next book in
Andrea Laurence's SECRETS OF EDEN miniseries,
A BEAUTY UNCOVERED, coming
October 2013 from Harlequin® Desire.*

Brody turned on his heel, ready to return to his office and lick his wounds, when she called out to him again.

"Mr. Eden?"

"Yes?" He stopped and faced her.

Sam rounded her desk and approached him. His body tensed involuntarily as she came closer. She reached up to the scarred side of his face, causing his lungs to seize in his chest. What was she doing?

"Your shirt…" Her voice drifted off.

He felt her fingertips gently brush the puckered skin along his neck before straightening his shirt collar. The innocent touch sent a jolt of heat through his body. It was so simple, so unplanned, and yet it was the first time a woman had touched his scars.

His foster mother had often kissed and patted his cheek, and nurses had applied medicine and bandages after various reconstructive procedures, but this was different. As a shiver ran down his spine, it *felt* different, as well.

Without thinking, he brought his hand up to grasp hers. Sam gasped softly at his sudden movement, but she didn't pull away when his scarred fingers wrapped around her own. He was glad. He wasn't ready to let go. His every nerve lit up with awareness, and he was pretty certain she felt it, too. Her dark brown eyes were wide as she looked at him, her moist lips parted seductively and begging for his kiss.

He slowly drew her hand down, his eyes locked on hers. Sam swallowed hard and let her arm fall to her side when he finally let her go. "Much better," she said, gesturing to his collar with a nervous smile. She held up the flash drive in her other hand. "I'll get this printed for you, sir."

"Call me Brody," he said, finding his voice when the air finally moved in his lungs again. He might still be her boss, but suddenly he didn't want any formalities between them. He wanted her to say his name. He wanted to reach out and touch her again. But he wouldn't.

Don't miss
A BEAUTY UNCOVERED by Andrea Laurence,
part of the Secrets of Eden miniseries, available
October 2013 from Harlequin® Desire.

HARLEQUIN®

Desire

YULETIDE BABY
SURPRISE

by *USA TODAY* bestselling author
Catherine Mann

The holiday spirit has professional rivals Miriama and
Rowan caring for an abandoned baby—together. But when
playing house starts to feel all too real, will they say yes to
becoming a family?

This Billionaires and Babies novel is also part of
Catherine Mann's series The Alpha Brotherhood.
Don't miss any of the excitement!

An Inconvenient Affair

All or Nothing

Playing for Keeps

All available now from Harlequin*® *Desire!

Powerful heroes…scandalous secrets…burning desires.

HD73270